ABOUT THE AUTHOR

Penny Freedman has taught Classics, English and Drama in a variety of schools, colleges and universities. She is also an actor and director. Her earlier books, *This is a Dreadful Sentence, All the Daughters, One May Smile, Weep a While Longer, Drown My Books* and *Little Honour,* featuring Gina and Freda Gray and DCI David Scott, are all published by Troubador.

CHRONICLES OF THE TIME

PENNY FREEDMAN

Matador
9 Priory Business Park,
Wistow Road, Kibworth Beauchamp,
Leicestershire. LE8 0RX
Tel: 0116 279 2299
Email: books@troubador.co.uk
Web: www.troubador.co.uk/matador
Twitter: @matadorbooks

ISBN 978 1800464 629

British Library Cataloguing in Publication Data.
A catalogue record for this book is available from the British Library.

Printed and bound in the UK by TJ Books Limited, Padstow, Cornwall
Typeset in 11pt Minion Pro by Troubador Publishing Ltd, Leicester, UK

Matador is an imprint of Troubador Publishing Ltd

This book is for my family and friends, whose text messages, emails, video clips, Zoom invitations, phone calls, doorstep drop-ins, shared walks and garden meetings were the bright moments during the monochrome months of isolation.

'They are the abstract and brief chronicles of the time.'
Hamlet on actors (Act 2, Scene 2)

Chapter One

WHATEVER IT TAKES

March 19th

In the days before we are officially locked down, confined to our homes to wait out the plague, I receive three phone calls in quick succession. One is from my granddaughter, Freda, one from my once best friend, and one from my ex-husband's current wife.

This last is the most surprising and it comes first. Barely has the PM finished his press conference, it seems to me, than my phone rings. Lavender is a sweet young woman – fond of children, kind to animals, not terribly bright. She is no match for Andrew in brains, bravura or bloody-mindedness. She and I have a reasonably comfortable relationship – she had nothing to do with my throwing Andrew out and although she may have assumed at first that I must be a thoroughly bad lot, ten years of marriage to Andrew has probably modified that view. My only problem with her is that she makes me feel guilty: I should not have released Andrew onto the marriage market before having *Not suitable for human relationships* tattooed somewhere on his person – preferably where it could be seen before someone went to bed with him. Better to nip it in the bud.

Today Lavender sounds bright and slightly febrile. 'Gina,' she says, 'I thought of you as soon as Boris made his announcement. How beastly, I thought, for people who live alone, and I know how much you enjoy company and I thought of you in a horrid flat in London for weeks on end, and so I wanted to say, do come and stay with us.'

I decide not to be offended by the *horrid flat*. My flat in Bloomsbury is, in fact, delightful, with a basement front entrance but a surprising little garden at the back from which light streams in. Lavender has never seen my flat, nor even had it described to her, I imagine. She just assumes that it is horrid because it is in London. Her family are local gentry and she grew up in a manor house in plush West Kent with ponies and dogs. She has done her best to replicate this with help from Daddy, and she and Andrew live in an impressive pile in the Kent countryside, known to my daughters and me as *Aren't-We-Grand Hall*. For Lavender, London means a trip to the West End for clothes shopping and possibly a show before returning to the clean air and birdsong of home. No-one, she thinks, would live in London unless they were forced to.

But what to say? My mind is sprinting towards an answer as she prattles on about lots of space and fresh air and lovely walks, playing with the children and walking the dogs. This invitation is not, of course, because she is concerned about me. At this particular moment, we are none of us concerned about anyone else really, are we? Our first reaction is to think about how we will get through it, what the ramifications are for us. So Lavender has thought about it and she has panicked. Fresh air and space or not, she is faced with weeks of isolation with an overbearing, inconsiderate husband, thwarted of the opportunities for triumph and plaudits that come to him as a successful lawyer, and with two small boys who will need to be home-schooled and who are, quite frankly, little monsters. If she has invited me to join her in her vision of purgatory, it is because she has grabbed hold of me in panic; I am, she thinks, the only person who might be able to manage Andrew, and possibly terrify the children too.

'What does Andrew say about the idea?' I ask.

'Oh, he's very happy about it.'

This cannot possibly be true. Andrew got himself a criminally good divorce deal on the grounds of my unreasonable behaviour.

'What did he say exactly, Lavender?'

'He said *Whatever you like,*' she says. 'He'll be working all the time, I expect, and I'm sure…'

Time to bring this to an end. 'It's a terribly kind thought, Lavender,' I say, 'and I do appreciate your thinking of me, but I shall be working. My students will still need to be taught so it will be non-stop online teaching and loads of preparation. So you see, I wouldn't be any sort of company, and I think Andrew might object to my heavy use of your broadband.'

'Oh, work, I hadn't thought of that,' she says. 'I thought your students would all just go home and —'

'They've paid a lot of money in fees.'

'Yes, of course.' She sounds deflated, then brightens. 'I might see if Mummy and Daddy would like to join us,' she says.

'Good idea,' I say. 'Lovely for them to spend time with the boys.'

'Yes.'

The brightness is already draining away. I must make my escape.

'Well, good luck with it all,' I say, and I am about to ring off when I hear myself adding, 'If you ever need to talk – unburden a bit, you know – you've got my number.'

Then I ring off, feeling guilty. This lockdown is going to be hard on women, isn't it? Domestic abuse will rocket. Men trapped at home, bored, scared, powerless, will drink too much and lash out, and women will have nowhere to go.

Andrew won't take to drink and he won't hit Lavender; he never hit me and I provoked him far more than Lavender ever could. But he can still make her life a misery. I know.

The next call, coming in the school lunch break, is from Freda, and she is refreshingly frank about her motives and priorities.

'Granny, I've got a mega favour to ask and if you say no I shall have to kill myself.'

I am alarmed, not by the rhetorical threat of self-slaughter but by fear of stepping out of line. I am on probation, you see, since a trip I took with Freda to the Lake District last summer culminated in a debacle spectacular enough to attract police intervention and media interest. No harm was actually done to Freda but her mother was terrified and I have not been allowed unsupervised access to Freda ever since. My daughter is now speaking to me again and before we started being stalked by the grim reaper of COVID-19, I had hoped that Freda would be permitted a visit to me for a few days of London delights during the Easter holidays. That is obviously not going to happen now but I want to feel that it will some time.

'Darling,' I say, 'you know that I would do anything for you, but don't ask me to do anything that will make your mum shout at me.'

'Oh, I've sorted things with her,' she says airily. 'She's cool with it.'

'And what is *it* exactly?'

'Me coming to stay with you for the lockdown. I can't stay here, Granny, I really can't. If I don't kill myself, I might kill somebody else.'

I have been aware of Freda's woes over the past weeks – she has rung me to offload several times. Essentially there is nothing wrong with Freda's life: her mother and stepfather love each other and love Freda and her little brother. Ben couldn't be a better stepfather and Freda loves him. She is bright, talented and healthy, goes to a good school and has friends. They live in the historic old town of Marlbury in Kent, which, though unexciting, is pleasant and safe. But her current dissatisfaction is not just irrational teenage angst; the problem is that three weeks ago, alarmed by the way the virus was cutting a swathe through the older generation in Italy, Ben brought his elderly Italian parents to live with them in their little house, so now *Nonna* and *Nonno* are occupying Freda's bedroom and she is sharing her seven-year-old brother's room. She is fond of her Italian step-grandparents but not having her own room is driving her round the bend.

'I keep thinking about my nice little room in your flat,' she says plaintively, 'and it feels like heaven.'

My nice little room is actually my study, I reflect, but of course I would like to have Freda here. Isn't that what I've been pining for? And yet…

'You know it won't be like it usually is, don't you?' I say. 'No shopping or theatre. And if we're allowed out it will be to walk round the streets.'

'I like walking round the streets. We can walk to the British Museum and back. And we can play Scrabble, even though you always win. And I'll bring Yahtzee.'

'It could be for three months, you know. Are you sure Mum is happy with it? How did you persuade her?'

'I made an irrefutable case.'

An irrefutable case. Oh, bless her. My heart is exploding with pride.

'Tell me,' I say.

'I just pointed out that we have a house with five rooms and there would be six people living and working there 24/7. Mum and Ben will have to do online teaching, so they'll need separate rooms, and my school is doing online classes so I'll need somewhere quiet, and Nico will need his room to play and learn in, and Nonna will probably be mostly in the kitchen, because that's where she always is, and Nonno will need their room (*my* room!) for his little naps, so there simply isn't enough space. A solution has to be found and I have found one.'

'And what did Mum say exactly?'

'She said it was fine.'

'Her words exactly?'

'Well, she said something like, *I suppose if she's not allowed to go anywhere, even Granny can't do too much damage.*'

'That sounds convincing. I'd love to have you here, darling. We could have a lovely time. But I ought to talk to Mum myself. I'll ring her this evening, OK?'

'Ace.'

There is the sound of a bell ringing at her end.

'Must go. Love you, Gran.'

And she is gone.

I go into my study and look at my desk, then go back into the living room to scan for a corner that I can set up as an office, but even as I am doing that, other priorities crowd in. Food. Supplies of all kinds. I have not really given this much consideration and when it was just going to be me here, the stories of panic buying and a toilet roll crisis didn't seem to matter. Now I have responsibilities. I will go out to Marks and Spencer's immediately and bring home whatever I can, but I will not panic. I sit down to make a list.

I have barely got started, though, when my phone rings again, and here is Irish Eve, who had a part to play in last summer's Lake District drama.

'How are you doing?' she asks.

'A bit bewildered, like everyone else,' I say, 'but hanging on in there. How about you?'

'Oh, I'm as cross as a camel,' she says.

'Why particularly? I mean, any more than the rest of us?'

'Have you heard of shielding?'

'As a term of art?'

'As in *everyone is locked down but you are super locked down*?'

'And what does that involve?'

'I am not allowed out at all – not even for a walk in the countryside.'

'Why?'

'My lungs.'

'The cough. Have you still got it?'

'Oh yes, I've still got it. And I share my house with a doctor who has explained in detail what the virus will do to my lungs.'

'So is *shielding* something Colin has dreamt up?'

'Oh no, it's a thing. We shall get letters, apparently, us with incompetent lungs and other failings, forbidding us to step outside our houses.'

'What a bugger.'

'So it is. But what I was thinking was, how would you like to come up and join me behind my shield? You would be allowed out, of course, as long as you didn't speak to anyone, and you'll have company. A gregarious woman like you needs people to organise – you'd not do well on your own. And we can offer lots of fresh air and empty fields, fresh vegetables from the garden, a well-stocked cellar and cards in the evenings.'

'It sounds idyllic, Eve,' I say quite sincerely, 'but Freda's coming to share my lockdown. Ben's parents are ensconced in Marlbury and Freda needs a bolthole. I'm just about to vacate my study.'

'But that's brilliant! Bring her. We've plenty of room. It would cheer me up no end to see her, and Colin will be pleased – he'll be missing his coaching. Some youth in the place is what we all need.'

It is tempting. I am a bit scared of the thought of Freda and me together possibly for months. What if we have a row

– it has been known – and neither of us has anywhere to go? What if we just get bored with each other? Our relationship might never recover.

'I don't know if Ellie –'

'Oh, Ellie! Has she agreed to Freda coming to you?'

'Yes. On the grounds that I can't do much harm if I'm not allowed out.'

'She doesn't know you well enough, does she? But seriously, I'll talk to Ellie if you like.'

'I need to talk to her anyway. I said I'd ring this evening.'

'Well, muster your arguments. The educational advantages. We'd be practically a school in ourselves with you for literature and languages, Colin for science – and he's pretty good with maths, too – and me for art.'

'I think you might be a bit tainted with what happened in the summer.'

'Well, point out that I took in two traumatised teenagers and coaxed them back to sanity and calm. What does Ellie want? Testimonials? I can get them if she likes.'

I laugh. 'I'm sure you could. I shall see what I can do first. And talk to Freda. She was imagining having me all to herself.'

'She'd soon get tired of that. Tell her that from me. And of course, the other girls will be up here.'

'She won't be able to see them, though, will she?'

'Well, I gather there's a plan among the young for synchronised dog walking. They plan to walk round the lake shouting to each other. Susan and I have two dogs from the same litter – puppies still, really. Flossie, ours is called. Wait till you see her – she'll be no match for Venetia's spaniels but she'll do her best.'

It interests me, on reflection, that all three of these invitations come via an old-fashioned phone call when we have so many zippier forms of communication – email, text,

WhatsApp, Facebook, and all the ones I don't know about. The phone call does what the others can't – it puts you on the spot, demands an immediate answer. If you really want to put the pressure on, the phone call is still the best option. I am out of practice at phone stalling, but as it happens, it doesn't matter. My fate was laid out for me: I was bound to say yes to Freda and to Eve, and it was always going to be no to Lavender.

And so it is that the following day finds me at St Pancras to meet Freda off the fast train from Marlbury. As it turned out, both she and Ellie agreed quite readily to the change of venue for our lockdown sojourn. Ellie, in fact, was quite eager, and I realised that she was actually hugely relieved to think that I wasn't going to be in sole charge and there would be some proper grown-ups taking responsibility for Freda. Freda herself was slightly more reluctant, unwilling to give up her happy fantasy of the two of us in our underground burrow, playing games and eating chocolate, but she likes Eve – rather hero-worships her, in fact, and I could get jealous – and the clincher was the prospect of seeing the girls with whom she bonded last summer: 'Synchronised dog walking sounds cool.'

At thirteen-and-a-half she has been trusted to do the fifty-five-minute journey unaccompanied and I have arrived ridiculously early, terrified that something might hold me up and I will fail in my responsibilities once again. When I spot her, she actually looks rather small to be travelling alone, but that is because she is burdened with luggage. She has a large-wheeled suitcase plus a laptop bag strung across her and what I take to be an art portfolio hanging from one shoulder. 'I brought everything,' she says breathlessly, 'because it could be months, couldn't it?' She looks doubtfully at my modest suitcase.

'I've taken a minimalist approach,' I say. 'I'm going to

keep the economy going with an orgy of online ordering. But I do have these.' I wave a Boots carrier bag. 'I found them in the shop here. The must-have gift for any hostess.'

'What are they?' she asks.

'Toilet rolls,' I say.

Chapter Two

CONTACTLESS DELIVERY

March 20th

Having Gary come to meet them at Penrith Station was now part of the pattern of visits to Carnmere, and Freda found the sight of him reassuring because she was a bit queasy about the strangeness of all this. Mainly it was exciting, and she was looking forward to time with Granny and seeing Eve and catching up with Grace and Ruby – and even Venetia – but it was strange not knowing how long this was going to go on for, and she didn't know Eve's husband, Colin. Milo and Fergus, his grandsons, loved him, she knew, but there was this mystery that hung about him – something he had done in the past when they were living in Marlbury. She knew it was to do with a girl being murdered, and that he was innocent really, but no-one was willing to talk about it properly. She couldn't help feeling that there would be something scary about him, but Granny and Eve would be there, wouldn't they? So nothing could be really that scary.

Gary didn't greet them with his usual friendly handshake but she was getting used to the no-touching regime – as they had all parted at school yesterday it had been bum bumps all round. In his very luxurious car Gary now had a glass screen behind his seat, separating him from his passengers, so it was more like being in a London taxi, and the inside of the car smelled strongly of sanitiser. Granny had to comment, of course.

'I see you're all prepared with your safety precautions, Gary,' she called through the glass.

'Only way I'm going to survive,' he called back. 'Who's going to want taxis? Only in emergencies, I reckon. If I can't keep some of my clients I shall go under.'

'There's going to be help from the Chancellor, isn't there? A statement on Monday, they said.'

'We'll see.' He sounded very unlike his usual cheery self. 'The self-employed usually come off worst.'

He drove on in silence and Granny didn't try any further conversation. It was evening rush hour time but the roads were oddly empty – it seemed that the lockdown had already begun. Freda felt gloom beginning to hover over them but as they came into the outskirts of Carnmere and there were its grey stone houses unlike any she had ever seen elsewhere, she felt a jolt of happy recognition. It was odd really because she hadn't always been happy while she was there, but it had been different and exciting and she had felt grown-up. As they cruised through the main square she saw the café where she and Mum had had a terrible row, and she supposed now that she had behaved badly. Perhaps she hadn't been as grown-up as she'd thought. Well, she was going to be perfectly grown-up now. She had asked Granny if she could spend the lockdown with her and she would not be a wimp now.

Eve's house was not far from the town centre and not far from the lake. It was in a terrace, its grey stone brightened by a tub of flaming geraniums on the doorstep. As Granny was paying Gary, Freda saw that she had added an extra ten pounds to the fare. 'Good luck, Gary,' she said. 'I'm not expecting adventures but I'll know where you are if I need you.' And he did at least smile.

The tall grey-haired man who opened the door to them was obviously Colin, and although he said "hello" perfectly pleasantly there was something not really welcoming about him. It wasn't just that there were no kisses or hugs, but the obvious distance he kept between himself and them. He stepped right back from the door to let them through and then stepped back further into the doorway of the kitchen, where a small black and white dog with a feathery tail was bouncing excitedly. As they stood rather helplessly occupying the little hall with their luggage, a door opened upstairs and Eve's voice called down.

'I'm sorry, my darlings, but I'm in solitary up here, I'm afraid. I hadn't quite thought through this part, but it won't last forever. Colin will explain.'

And Colin did explain, sounding very like a doctor and talking to Granny, ignoring Freda. 'Eve is highly vulnerable,' he said. 'She has a lung disease – alveolitis – probably the result of all the materials she has used in her work over the years. She can't afford to risk getting COVID-19 so –'

Granny interrupted. 'We know that, Colin. Eve has explained about the shielding.'

'But,' he glanced up at the landing, where Eve must have been standing, though Freda couldn't see her, 'what Eve didn't think about is what happens now. You two have just come off public transport. I imagine that Freda was at school yesterday. You are at the moment a threat to Eve's life.'

Freda felt herself going red, as though she was guilty of something and had been caught out.

Granny said, 'So would you like us to turn round and go home?'

Did she mean that seriously? At that moment, Freda rather hoped that she did.

Colin was startled too, she thought. He ran a hand over his eyes as though he was trying to change the picture in front of them. 'Of course not,' he said. 'You simply have to be quarantined.'

'Which means what?'

'We all stay in our own rooms. Eve is using the shed as a studio and she'll be there a good deal of the time. You two have plenty of work to do, I imagine – it is still term time, after all – and you will be able to do that in your rooms. You will have use of the bathroom; Eve and I will use our en suite. We will eat separately. We can arrange timing for use of the kitchen.'

Granny bent down to stroke the dog, who had apparently not yet been trained in the social distancing rules. 'What about exercise, Colin?' she asked. 'Freda was looking forward to walking the dog.'

'She can do that, as long as we sanitise the lead handle afterwards.'

'And how long does this go on for?'

'Fourteen days is the official quarantine period, but the fourteen-day incubation cases seem to be statistical outliers. I'm satisfied with ten days.'

Freda looked at her grandmother, who looked back. They were both, they knew, considering whether to summon Gary back and return to London. Then Eve's voice came down to them again.

'It's about the worst welcome you could have and I wouldn't blame you for walking out. I am so sorry, and I'm sorry Colin is being so doctorish about it.'

Granny came to a decision. Freda could see it happening as she watched her face. Granny called up to Eve, angling herself round so that she could see up the stairs.

'Colin's just looking after you, my love, but it is a bit unexpected and I need to talk to Freda because it's her lockdown too, so we'll just step outside for a moment to confer.'

She opened the front door and Colin came out of the kitchen and said quietly, in a voice that was less official and pompous, 'I'm really not trying to be difficult, Gina, and it would make all the difference to Eve having you and Freda here.'

The house had no front garden so they walked up and down the pavement having their conversation.

'How do you feel about it?' Granny asked.

'I really don't know. You want to stay, don't you?'

'I'd like to help Eve, but I want us two to enjoy ourselves too. You took a big step leaving Mum and Ben and Nico, and I want you to be happy. It really is up to you.'

'Is Colin always like that?'

'He's worried – and he's embarrassed, I think. It's going to be difficult to adjust to the new normal. Usually we're too polite to treat people as a health hazard, even if they turn up at our house with a streaming cold. It's hard to be impolite.'

'How long do you think we'll be here, honestly?' Freda asked.

'This will go on for at least three months, I think. We're not expecting our students back for the summer term, and there's talk of cancelling GCSE and A-level exams.'

'And do you think once the ten days are over it will be OK?'

'Well, you know Eve. Once we can see her, it—'

'But what about him? How will he be? Because I'm not really up for months of being ordered about.'

'I'm with you there. But he's a nice man, really. We just caught him at a bad moment.'

They had reached the end of the road and had paused, uncertain whether to carry on or turn round.

'I tell you what,' Granny said, 'why don't you ring Ruby and ask her? She has chemistry coaching with him, doesn't she? Ask her what he's like.'

'OK.'

She got out her phone and as she scrolled down for Ruby's number she walked back in the direction of the house, her grandmother tactfully waiting where she was.

'Are you here?' Ruby asked.

'We are, but it's all a bit weird.'

When she had explained about the quarantine and, with more difficulty, about how off-putting Colin had been – how she felt, in fact, that he might expect her to call him *Dr Fletcher* – Ruby said, 'He is actually really kind. And funny. I know what you mean about him at the moment – he cancelled our last lesson and he was quite rude. I think he called me a *potential source of contamination*. Grace has a theory. She says he still misses being a doctor and now he has just one patient so he's overdoing it.'

'Do you think he'll be all right once we've been quarantined? Will he mind the synchronised dog walks? I do like the dog, by the way. She seems sweet.'

'You'll like Boris too.'

'You haven't called your dog Boris?'

'Afraid so. Because his fringe hangs in his eyes. And just don't tell Colin about the synchronising. Offer to do a regular morning walk and we'll fit in with you. There's a great walk round the lake and no tourists so it's empty. Some mornings Grace and I sing!'

'OK. You've sold it,' Freda said. 'The singing clinches it.'

'Half past nine tomorrow morning at the jetty. Love you.'

She rang off. Freda stood for a moment, looking at her phone, then she turned and beckoned her grandmother back towards the house.

When Colin answered the door to them for the second time, Granny said, 'You knew we'd stay, didn't you?' as she stepped over the threshold.

'You've never been a quitter, Ms Gray,' he said. 'Please

consider yourselves warmly embraced.' He looked at Freda. 'Both of you.'

Freda wondered if Eve had given him a quick lesson in charm while they had been outside.

Directed upstairs to their rooms, they found WELCOME TO YOUR NEW HOME signs on the doors, written in Eve's best calligraphy, and the rooms themselves were sweet, side by side, looking out over the garden. Granny offered her the bigger room.

'You'll need space for your art stuff. When we're spending time together up here, we'll spend it in your room because you're tidier than I am. Is that OK?'

'Compared with sharing a room with Nico, it's heaven.'

And compared with her little room in Granny's flat? She wouldn't think about that. There would be other times for that. And in spite of lockdown, she couldn't help feeling that this was a place for an adventure.

Once her grandmother had gone next door, she looked round her room, deciding how to arrange things. There was a table under the window with a mirror standing on it, so it was obviously supposed to be a dressing table, but she thought she would move the mirror and use the table as a desk. What she looked like wasn't going to be important anyway, was it, if she was going out only to walk the dog? Grace could look glam, she was sure, being at a stage school, but she and Ruby wouldn't be glamming up for tramping round the lake, surely.

She put her suitcase on the bed and lifted out the clothes she had brought – not many, in fact, because she had needed the space for school books, and Granny had said they could do online buying for summer stuff if they ended up staying that long. She put away what she had in the little painted cupboard in the corner and then piled up books on the table with her laptop. The book she was currently reading was half a school book really as they were doing Elizabethan England in history.

It was called *The Young Elizabeth* and she had found it in the school library. It was quite old and she noticed that nobody had taken it out for ages, but she liked it. This was the kind of history she liked – about interesting people, not the *everyday life of a sheep farmer's family* stuff, which was incredibly boring.

She had just finished arranging everything and was looking for somewhere to stow her suitcase when there was a knock at the door and Granny stood there holding a bottle of whiskey, a large box from Hotel Chocolat and a mammoth pack of toilet rolls.

'I'm going to leave these on the hall table,' she said. 'I've written a note.'

Freda looked at the piece of paper balanced on top of the chocolates. It was more a notice than a note, she thought, written in red felt tip: *FOR YOU. SANITISE AS REQUIRED.* Freda thought Colin would not find it funny.

'Help me take these down,' Granny said, 'then I'll tell you about supper.'

Freda felt that they almost had to creep down the stairs. They could hear voices in the kitchen but the door was closed and they retreated upstairs to Granny's room, which was already messier than Freda's.

Granny said, 'I've had a phone conversation with Eve – that's how we're to communicate, it seems. They're having their supper now but Eve has made us a lasagne and we can have it when they've finished. We'll have an explore of the kitchen then too – look at the stores. Eve says we're getting deliveries from the farm shop, and there are Colin's vegetables – cabbage, leeks and carrots mainly, I think. I feel we're going to need some luxuries so I'm going to explore online deliveries as our contribution.'

Freda sat on the bed and looked at the books on the bedside table, both fat volumes – one huge, in fact.

'Are these fiction?' she asked.

'Historical fiction but seriously researched. I'm living in Tudor England with these two.'

'We're doing the Tudors but I don't like the everyday life stuff.'

'Well, the big one – *The Mirror and the Light* – is high politics and royalty. It's about Thomas Cromwell. Have you come across him?'

'I think… yes – we watched the film *A Man for All Seasons*. He's in that, isn't he? He's Thomas More's enemy.'

'Oh, that film. Paul Schofield being the saintly Sir Thomas.'

'Wasn't he saintly?' Freda asked.

Granny brandished her book. 'This writer makes him a self-righteous creep and a sadistic religious extremist. In her view, Thomas Cromwell is the hero.'

'So who is right?' Freda asked. 'Historically, I mean. What's the truth?'

Her grandmother shrugged. 'We don't know. We can't know. All we have is what people have said or written, and they always have an agenda. Think about how two people on either side of the Brexit debate would give *the facts*. They would be entirely different, wouldn't they? And when the story of Brexit is written in a history book, how it's told will depend partly on whether it turns out to be a good idea or a bad one.'

'But the facts would be the same. Facts are facts.'

'Two things: one, it depends which facts you report and which you leave out, and two, sometimes facts aren't facts at all – they are just not true.'

'So how do people know in history what is true and what isn't?'

'Quite often they don't. Some things are recorded at the

time, like what laws were passed and when someone became king or queen, but even something like who won a battle isn't clear – sometimes both sides claimed to have won.'

'Then what's the point of learning history?'

'Good question. The point ought to be that there's always another side to any story, but mostly the history you learn at school about your own country is teaching you the story that we want to believe. There's a saying that history is written by the victors. The Tudors are a good example. Henry VIII's father had an extremely dodgy claim to the throne and he won it by invading England with a foreign army, so he had to set up the idea that Richard III, who he turfed off the throne, was a murdering tyrant. He did it very well – helped, by the way, by the saintly Sir Thomas More and then by Shakespeare – so now everyone believes that Richard was a hunchbacked villain who murdered his two little nephews.'

'Well, didn't he?'

'Quite possibly not. It may well have been Henry VII who got rid of them.'

'It makes me feel quite dizzy,' Freda said. She picked up the other book that lay beside the bed. '*Hamnet*,' she said. 'What's this one about?'

'It's about Shakespeare's son, who was called Hamnet.'

'Like *Hamlet*?'

'Yes, they're variations of the same name. Hamnet died when he was eleven. We don't know what he died of, but the writer imagines that it was the plague – topical for now, of course – and she imagines the life of his family and how they cope with his death. Hamnet had a twin sister, so there's a lot about her too. It's not history, but Maggie O'Farrell has done lots of research and she gives a brilliant picture of their lives. It's the sort of *everyday life* that you would like.'

'Would I like the book?'

'Not yet, I think. It is so sad – beautifully sad, but I don't think now is the time for you to go there.'

'Did Shakespeare write *Hamlet* before or after Hamnet died?'

'A few years after. In the book, she imagines that he wrote it for Hamnet. The play is all about fathers and sons.'

Freda put down the book and said, 'I'll stick with *The Young Elizabeth* for the moment, though I suppose you'll tell me none of it is true.'

They went downstairs to eat their lasagne, and Freda recorded in her diary before she went to bed: *A nice evening. Delicious veggie lasagne. Granny alarmed by lack of Marmite. On an online order mission. Played Scrabble (I won but Granny played with 6 tiles) and Yahtzee (I won). All a bit weird but OK. A bit like camping. V quiet with no traffic. Apparently most of history isn't true. Should I mention this to Mrs Yardley in our Zoom History lesson? Rang Mum.*

Chapter Three

QUARANTINE

March 21ˢᵗ

It is 00.01, as indicated on my laptop, when I win the jackpot in the online delivery lottery. When I decided to order food for us online, I was in cloud cuckoo land. I had no idea of the realities of life as we now know it. It is not a field in which I am an expert anyway. I have in fact ordered an online delivery only once before. I don't usually have any reason to – I live in an area of London stuffed with food shops from multiple cultures – but on that occasion I had invited people to a party and then run out of shopping time. It was fine, except that the pictures on screen didn't reflect the size of the product and I hadn't paid close attention to the weight information, so I ended up with an enormous bag of carrots when I wanted only enough for a few crudités, and a very small tub of guacamole for us to fight over. However, I felt I understood the principle, and in bed last night I opened up my laptop and googled the upmarket provider I had used before. When I was confronted by red messages warning me off attempting to get any food from them, I went downmarket and got the same response. They were, I could see, simply laughing at me for thinking that I could sail in at this point and actually purchase anything. I was not prepared to give in, though, and steeled myself to go back and look at the small print, and there I found on one of the sites, in extremely small print, an admission that they released new delivery slots at midnight. I logged on before midnight, of course, and had to watch as a little green lorry icon crawled across my screen, indicating my place in the queue, but here I am with my slot – though when I say I have hit the jackpot, I have to tell you that my order is scheduled for between six and seven in the morning in five days' time.

I said I wasn't an expert, and now I see that I should have made a list beforehand. Now I am being told that I have only fifteen minutes to complete my order before it disappears into the ether, and my mind has gone blank. I have ordered a large pot of Marmite and two packets of muesli since I noticed the absence of those in the kitchen, and I have just added bottles of diet Coke, bananas and blueberry yoghurts, which were Freda's requests, but I am stuck now. The larder seems to be well stocked with basics and I dare not order fruit and veg for fear of seeming to disparage local produce, so what else do we need? Am I really doing this simply for the sake of a jar of Marmite? Treats are what we need to see us through, so I order six bottles each of Valpolicella and prosecco, which takes me over the minimum spend limit, and add two boxes of salted caramel fudge and two tubs of luxury ice cream. *Who knows when I shall get another slot?* I think, and add a third tub. I also add avocados – surely Colin can't be offended by those – as avocado toast is good lunch food and we can't eat baked beans every day. Toast makes me think about baking. I expect the farm shop will deliver bread and hearty cakes and biscuits if asked, but I have a picture of us baking together, the sunny kitchen full of the smells of warm sugar and spices. I search for flour and find that everyone else has had the same idea; the virtual shelves are virtually bare. I believe, though, that I have managed to secure one of the last bags of self-raising flour in captivity – organic, artisan and expensive. How come every working mother in the country believes that if she had more time at home, she would spend it making cakes? How did baking become so virtuous?

I add lemons and parmesan because there is hardly any dish that isn't improved by the addition of one or both of them, and at this point invention deserts me and I take my trolley to the checkout and pay. I am informed that I can add to my order during the next three days but I don't really believe it.

After this I am wide awake, of course, and spend a long time with Thomas Cromwell, watching him losing his footing on the greasy floors of Henry's court, and I seem to have slept hardly at all when Freda knocks on my door. She edges in bearing two mugs of tea.

'I met Colin as I was going to the bathroom,' she says by way of explanation. 'He was on his way to make tea for Eve and he offered to make us some.'

'I didn't know you'd started drinking tea,' I say, sitting up and accepting my mug.

'It's herbal.'

'Yuk. I hope mine isn't.' I sniff apprehensively.

'No. He gave me a choice.'

'You seem to have had quite a conversation. Did you use a megaphone?'

Over the top of her mug she gives me a look that I can't quite read. 'He was halfway down the stairs. He said thank you for the presents, by the way.'

I sip my tea, which is encouragingly strong.

'What flavour is yours?' I ask.

'Lemon, ginger and ginseng. It wakes you up.'

'Not as much as caffeine does, I bet.'

'I may have to report you to Mum as a bad influence.'

'Don't joke! I'm still on probation.'

I grope around for my phone. 'What time is it? I did the

online order, by the way, and it demanded all my nerve and guile.'

'Did you remember the yoghurts?'

'I did, but it's not coming till Thursday – first thing in the morning. I'm relying on you to be up. Do you always bounce out of bed this early?'

'It's seven forty-five and I'm meeting Grace and Ruby at eight thirty.'

'Right. Down for breakfast in fifteen minutes then. Did you discuss breakfast times with Colin?'

'He's taking a tray up for Eve. We can go down any time.'

'And he's happy for us to take Flossie out?'

'Us?' She is at the door now, about to leave, but she turns round. 'I thought the dog walking was just for the three of us.'

'Sorry, no.' I swing my legs out of bed. 'I'm serious about being on probation. I can't risk any mishaps. I'll be chaperoning, I'm afraid. I'm happy to hold back and trail along behind you but I need to have you in my sights at all times.'

I am aiming for the kind of no-nonsense, cheerful bossiness that Eve always manages so well. I don't think I'm altogether successful but she doesn't argue.

'Whatever,' she says and goes out.

Last summer, when she hit thirteen, she seemed to be showing all the symptoms of Year Nine Syndrome – the uncertain oscillation between childishness and assertive claims to adultness, the moods, the air of sullen resentment. I realised later that she had good reasons for some of this, and now I think she has mainly come through it and is heading for being a rather nice teenager. And she seems to be able to negotiate with Colin, which lets me off the hook. And perhaps, like the rest of us, she realises that if we are all going to be shut up together here, we can none of us afford to have moods.

It takes about ten minutes to walk to the jetty where we are meeting the girls, and our route takes us through the town square, where the shoppers are surely out earlier than they would be on a normal Saturday morning. Those bulging bags are evidence of panic buying, I think censoriously, before reminding myself of my own midnight retail frenzy. *Three tubs of ice cream? Really?* I formulate a variation on the classic syllogism:

> *I am making sensible provision.*
> *You are going over the top.*
> *She is panic buying.*

There is certainly an absence in town today of the relaxed, weekend shopping-for-pleasure vibe; people look as grim-faced and determined as they do on the weekend before Christmas.

At the jetty, Grace and Ruby are waiting for us, and when we stop at the obligatory two-metre distance, they semaphore greetings and go into an exaggerated mime of virtual hugging and air kissing. Freda giggles and responds with a modified version – she is not really a performer. The dogs, exempt from government restrictions, greet each other ecstatically and intimately. They are brother and sister and they seem to remember this, checking out one another's recent activities by sniffing very thoroughly at both ends.

Grace says, 'Venetia and Letty won't be back from school till later today, so it's just us this morning,' and we set off in convoy, with Boris, the Buxtons' dog, leading the way along the lakeside path, Ruby holding his lead, Flossie straining to catch up and restrained by Freda, and me hanging back, trying to be unobtrusive. Grace, who is a bundle of energy, dances along beside Ruby, throwing questions and information over her shoulder to Freda at first, and then settling on a method of facing Freda by walking backwards while holding on to Ruby's arm for guidance.

They start with an exchange of views on what sucks about the lockdown: Ruby complains that her teachers have just set them masses of work to do but there are no plans for online teaching; Freda says she should think herself lucky – her school is doing back-to-back Zoom classes and she's going to be looking at a screen all day; Grace says she was supposed to be singing Anita in *West Side Story* at the end of term and now she's lost her chance.

'On the other hand,' she says, 'I get to be here with Rube and Boris and you, when Saturday mornings at school involve a nine o'clock ballet class.' And then she turns about to put her arm round Ruby and breaks into a rendition of *A Boy Like That*. When she has finished, she says, 'Sorry, I just have to sing when I'm out here – it's the only place where I can really open my lungs. I feel inhibited in the house.'

I am amazed at this girl. She is fifteen and just last month she gave evidence (by video link, it is true) against her father, who was in court, charged with abusing her and attempting to kill her mother. And yet she looks glowing with health and wellbeing, singing her heart out as though the world had only good to offer her. The counselling she has been given at her stage school in Oxfordshire must be remarkably good. Unless all the hurt has been buried deep, of course, and this is an extremely skilled performance.

'Actually,' Grace says, 'my friends and I are planning to do a YouTube video of life-affirming songs to put out as a lockdown cheer-up. So if you have any requests, let me know.'

'What have you got so far?' I call from my station in the rear.

Grace numbers them on her fingers. '*Oh What a Beautiful Morning, Climb Every Mountain, There's a Place for Us,*

Somewhere Over the Rainbow, I Will Survive, You'll Never Walk Alone. That's all so far, so we could do with a few more.'

'How about *Jerusalem*?' I say. 'Or is that too solemn?'

'Oh excellent! In fact,' she nudges Ruby, 'we should sing it now. Do you sing, Freda?'

'I'm in the choir at school,' Freda says, 'but—'

'Ace! OK then, *one, two, three…*' and she launches in, with Ruby just a beat behind and Freda coming in on the second line. You can hear that Grace's voice has been trained – it has real body – while Ruby's and Freda's are sweet and true but are still the voices of children. Between them they make me cry, and it is as I turn away to wipe away the tears with my sleeve that I see the man. He is standing under a tree beside the path and the first thing I notice about him is that he is smoking. You very rarely see that now, do you? It can't be illegal to smoke in the open air, I imagine, but I suppose public censure keeps it under control. I can remember a time in the early '90s when I used to walk through Marlbury town centre to the station in the early morning to catch a train out to the college I taught at in Thanet, on the eastern edge of Kent, and the aroma of people's early morning nicotine hits hung in a cloud over the high street. I don't get that now, in London, on my way to work. So the cigarette amidst the lakeside greenery looks oddly out of place, but there is something else odd about him too – his stillness, and the fixed way he is regarding the girls. He has a hungry look and I don't like it at all.

Without making it too obvious, I hope, I try to take in his appearance so I could give a description of him if I had to, but there is nothing distinctive and he has his anorak hood up. There is nothing sinister in that – it is a chilly morning and I have mine up – but it means that all I see is a man of medium height, neither old nor young, with a look on his face that I don't care for.

The girls haven't even noticed him, I think, and I know that, though I joked with Freda about never letting her out of my sight because I am on probation with Ellie, I am not sure that they would be safe out alone in the weeks to come, not even with the dubious protection of Flossie and Boris. It may sound apocalyptic, but being female is going to be a perilous business in the coming weeks – abuse given free rein behind the locked-down doors and stranger danger rampant in the deserted streets and fields.

Happily unaware, Grace and Ruby have switched to *Oh What a Beautiful Morning* as we move on round the lake. A young woman comes past us, jogging, from the other direction and I hope that the man will have gone before she gets to those trees.

Eventually we turn back ourselves – walking all round the lake would be a half-day trek – and we part at the jetty with a promise to reconvene the next day. Back at home, Freda and I hand Flossie over to Colin for sanitisation and go upstairs to our rooms. Freda needs to refresh her social contacts and I need to work out how to organise online seminars across four continents.

At our last department meeting, last week, various options for completing the academic year were discussed. The bulk of group teaching has been done now, in fact, and officially there is only one more week of term to go. Next term our students will be writing their dissertations and it will be a matter of organising individual tutorials via Skype, Zoom or other more exotic communication apps as yet unknown to me. For the moment, though, I have to organise my students' practice for their assessed presentations next term. The students' presentations this week are by way of a mock exam for the real thing. It will be odd for them to give them online, but then the assessed ones will be done online too. The department discussion meandered inconclusively but the outcome for me was clear: I am on my own. I have an obligation to make sure that my students complete the work of the term but how I achieve this is up to me.

I am not a technophobe or a Luddite, but I am not very interested in it all and I am in the habit of taking anything technically challenging to our nice, helpful tech support chaps at work. Now I am afraid of making a fool of myself and looking old and stupid. I am quite used to Skyping with individual students who get extensions on writing their dissertations and complete them in their home countries after their visas expire, but I am told that Zoom is best for group communication – simple and stable, I am told, though also easily hacked, so I have to be stringent about requiring IDs and passwords. I did experience a practice Zoom meeting last week, and that was fine, but then I wasn't the one convening the meeting.

My first stumbling block is the discovery that I will have to pay for unlimited time because the basic app offers only forty-five minutes, and I require a hefty two hours. Will the college reimburse me? Possibly. After that, though, it is actually quite straightforward, and the most difficult thing is working out appropriate timing. My group of twelve students started dispersing more than a week ago, heading for their native countries before the doors slammed shut, so they are now scattered from east to west – from Honshu to Bogotá, in fact – and I can't expect anyone to be attending class in the middle of the night. I am obviously going to have to do two sessions, and I settle on one at nine in the morning, my time, to catch the Far East students before they feel that the working day is over, and one in the late afternoon to catch the South American students as soon as they wake up. The European and African students can take their pick. I set up the meetings, send out the invitations and, feeling inordinately pleased with myself, I bounce into Freda's room to announce my success. She is sitting at the table under the window, intent on her laptop.

'I have sent out invitations to Zoom meetings to students on four continents,' I announce.

She does not turn round and continues to focus on her screen while she says, 'So which ones didn't you do?'

'What?'

'Which continents?'

This is not the response I was looking for. 'Well, Antarctica, obviously,' I say, 'and I don't teach Australian or North American students because they speak English already.'

'Right,' she says, and that seems to be that. I creep downstairs to make coffee and raid the biscuit tin.

As I am waiting for the kettle to boil, I look out of the window into the garden. I can see Eve moving around in her shed/workshop not far from the house and beyond that I can see Colin among his vegetables – weeding, it looks like, but I am no expert. I put my coffee on a tray with two bourbon biscuits. They used to be a staple in school staff rooms and I haven't had one since I gave up that sort of teaching.

Upstairs, I have just settled down to my coffee and my emails when my phone rings.

'Ground control to Major Tom,' a voice says.

I look out of the window and there is Eve, on her phone, standing in the doorway of her shed.

'I saw you in the kitchen so I knew you weren't working,' she says. 'How are you doing?'

'I've arranged international online teaching sessions and Freda has failed to be impressed.'

She laughs. 'Of course she's not impressed. That stuff is mother's milk to them. I'm impressed, anyway. I can't do any of that stuff – it's Colin who does the Skyping with the grandkids.'

'How are you doing? Feeling creative?'

'Not really. This is the time when I'm usually piling up the work to sell over the spring and summer but I can't see that happening, and my stuff isn't exactly art for art's sake these days.'

'Maybe lay in stuff for Christmas then? Do you sell much then?'

'I have a stall at the market but that's all cosy stuff – candle holders and such. I can't make those now – the vibes are all wrong. I want to do *daisies pied and violets blue*. What poem does that come from?'

'It's *Love's Labour's Lost* – the final song. Anyway, give it a few days and we can be idle together. My term finishes at the end of this coming week, so as soon as Colin lets me out of quarantine we can watch old films and eat ice cream. I've done an online order with a few treats, by the way.'

'What did you get?'

I reel off the contents of my virtual trolley and she goes into peals of laughter. 'I don't suppose the youngsters who collect up the stuff for the deliveries bother to speculate about their customers,' she says, 'but they might worry about you!'

'They don't know about the farm shop – or the garden produce.'

'Oh yes, do eat the garden produce. Colin leaves it in a box in the kitchen. Take whatever you like. He'll be so pleased.'

'I'll make a *tutto giardino* sauce this evening. I don't suppose you have farfalle among your pasta stores?'

'Don't think so. What shape are they?'

'Butterflies. I feel they go with the garden sauce, but any pasta will do. I'd be happy to make it for you too, but I don't suppose Colin will allow that.'

'Afraid not, but I'll look forward to an encore when we're allowed.'

'I've noticed that there are plenty of eggs. Is it all right if I make scrambled eggs for us for lunch?'

'Please do. The hens at the farm seem to have gone into lockdown overdrive and Tom is overproviding. What are you doing this afternoon?'

'I think I'll settle down with *The Mirror and the Light.*'

'Ah. Isn't it a great feeling to start in on a nice fat book that you know you're going to enjoy?'

'Sometimes I think it's the best feeling in the world.'

Eve laughs. 'I'd still choose cuddling a new baby,' she says.

At lunch time I don't angle any more for praise from Freda but ask politely what she has been doing.

'Catching up,' she says. 'Loads of stuff from school – classes for next week. Mrs Yardley has sent us pictures of the Globe Theatre.'

'You're doing the Elizabethan theatre?'

'Just starting on it. We were going on a trip to see the Globe in London next week so the pictures are instead.'

'Have you ever seen the film *Shakespeare in Love*? That's all about Elizabethan theatre.'

'Comedy or tragedy?'

'Oh, it's a romcom. We could see if we can download it and watch it on one of our laptops if you like.'

She hesitates.

'I promise not to give any lectures,' I say.

'In that case, OK.' She jumps up. 'Do you think it's all right if I go and play with Flossie in the garden? She's standing there looking so hopeful with that ball in her mouth.'

'I'm sure it's all right. Just don't go and breathe on Eve.'

I clear up our lunch things and then go back upstairs with a cup of coffee, which I drink while standing at my window, watching Freda and Flossie. Flossie is wildly excited about having the ball thrown for her but she hasn't cottoned on to bringing it back so Freda is chasing her for it. She looks terribly young as she charges round, laughing. Well, thirteen is young, and now I am having qualms about *Shakespeare in Love*. It is a long time since I saw it, but isn't it actually more about sex than theatre? Are we going to be embarrassed watching it together? Would Ellie disapprove? I can at least demonstrate what a responsible grandmother I am being. I pick up my phone and send a rapid text.

Too much sex in Shakespeare in Love for Freda? Designed to be educational. They are doing Eliz theatre. Will take your advice xx

There! Exemplary, I would say. I get a swift reply, which surprises me – Ellie can hardly be at a loose end with Zoom classes to prepare, Nico to amuse and Nonna and Nonno under her feet. Her text is brief and clear.

Wouldn't show it to a class cos too much sniggering but F will cope. Just don't try to explain the literary jokes xx

As if I would!

As I am watching the scene below, my eyes travel beyond to the garden that backs onto this one. A young woman is crouched on the ground near the end of the garden, deep in conversation with a tabby cat, and the cat is weaving around, rubbing itself against her in that tarty way cats have. Then, down the garden comes a man who shouts "Oi" and claps loudly, sending the cat up the nearest tree. The woman, I notice, doesn't protest but stays crouching on the ground. I am really interested now and press my nose to the window for a better look. The man puts out a hand to her and pulls her to her feet, and though I couldn't say that he drags her up, there is something more commanding than helpful in the gesture, and as they go up the garden towards the house, he puts an arm round her shoulders and seems to steer her. It's not forceful enough to be called coercive, but there is something about it I don't quite like. It makes me uneasy.

Shakespeare in Love is a success. I am true to my word about lecturing and explaining jokes, though I do explain at the outset that Kit Marlowe was the young Shakespeare's greatest rival – Cambridge-educated, whereas Shakespeare was just a grammar school boy, and better known. Freda seems not to be embarrassed by the sex scenes, but she does ask for a pause at one point and asks, 'So why, exactly, weren't women allowed to be actors?'

'It was thought improper for women to display themselves in public like that,' I say, too glibly.

'Why improper?'

'Well, you read your historical romances, don't you? You know what restrictions there were on what women could do. They belonged to their fathers until they married, and then to their husbands. If they did anything that wasn't respectable before they married, they lost their market value as wives, and anything they did afterwards reflected on their husbands.'

'But why was acting not respectable?'

'It was a rackety sort of life – insecure, touring round. Players weren't gentlemen. But there's a specific thing about women on stage. They are being looked at – by a mostly male audience – and most men can't look at a woman without thinking about sex. Keeping women off the stage wasn't to protect them, though. It was to stop men from having lewd thoughts and endangering their souls. It's the same with making women wear veils.'

She looks sceptical. I used to be a fount of wisdom, but these days she doesn't necessarily believe what I say. 'OK,' she says. 'Let's watch the rest.'

It's an odd romcom, of course, with no possibility of a

conventional happy ending, and perhaps that is why I feel jumpy and unsettled and can't get to sleep. I lie in the dark and try one of my settling strategies – an audit of the day's achievements and failures. This can work but it is chancy: if the former outnumber the latter, the result can be happiness, but if the reverse is the case, the result is the other thing. Tonight, the achievements column looks good: didn't spoil the girls' walk, didn't laugh at Colin's sanitising the dog lead, sent out Zoom invitations, cooked excellent pasta, introduced Freda to Elizabethan theatre. Against these, in the failures column, are my sins of omission: didn't contact David, didn't contact Annie. These are recurrent items on the list. I will ring them both tomorrow, really. But achievements and failures are not enough – there are also the anxieties, and these are what are keeping me awake. I make myself list them too. *When the other girls join us tomorrow, can I safely supervise our unwieldy caravan? Will the man under the trees be there again? Is the woman in the house behind ours being bullied? And what about the cat?*

Chapter Four

WASH YOUR HANDS

March 28th

So first Prince Charles had the virus and now Boris Johnson had it. The heir to the throne and the prime minister. As Granny said, if this was a disaster movie you would say the writers were overdoing it. What Colin said when they had their usual early morning exchange as she came down to collect their mugs of tea was, *Well, that's what comes of shaking hands.*

Apart from these public dramas, life in quarantine was really going rather well, especially the morning walks, which Grace was turning into street performance – or path performance, anyway. It turned out that Venetia and Letty could sing too, and every day of the past week Grace had emailed them the words of the next morning's song so they could learn them. And every morning there seemed to be a few more people walking the path, as if they were there for the entertainment. In normal times, she thought, people would have been annoyed by it and called it showing off, but something odd had happened since the lockdown: everyone seemed to have gone into a weird sort of cheerfulness, and things that adults used to moan about had suddenly become *community spirit*. So children had covered walls and pavements with chalk rainbows and instead of complaining about graffiti, people were smiling and saying *How lovely*, and there were wool pompoms beginning to appear on trees, and Facebook was full of videos of kittens and puppies and babies doing cute things. So, instead of telling them to behave themselves when they marched along singing, people smiled and even clapped – apart from the scary man who was there most days, standing under the trees, smoking his cigarette and looking as though he never smiled at anything.

The walk was the best part of the day, of course, because the Zoom classes were quite tedious since all the teachers seemed to be able to do was to talk at them and then set them work to do. They had tried a discussion in an English class but when everyone unmuted you could hear all the noises from their homes, and people didn't put their hands up so everyone was talking at once. And now she had to think about two projects – one for Art and one for History. Granny said it was lazy teaching, setting projects, but she quite liked the idea. In art, the project was to create a set of pictures that showed the effect of the lockdown on familiar places. No-one was going to be able to sit outside and sketch, though, so it was going to have to be a matter of noticing and remembering. For History, they could choose any aspect of Elizabethan England to write about, which was so broad it was difficult to know where to start. If she asked Granny or Mum for advice, they would probably both suggest the Elizabethan theatre, but what she wanted was to write about an interesting person. More than that, she wanted to write about a person with a mystery attached to them. Perhaps it was being with Granny that made her think about mysteries, but that was what she wanted.

At lunch time – they were eating smashed avocado on toast for the third day running because Granny's food delivery had arrived two days before, bringing six ripe avocadoes, and it seemed that Eve and Colin weren't eating them – Freda broached the subject of the History project.

'So I'd like to write about a mystery,' she said. 'I think it would be interesting to research it and I've been thinking about what you said about nobody knowing the truth about history. That means you can imagine, doesn't it?'

'Well, speculate, anyway. I'm not sure that you could get away with fiction – like your historical romances. But a history mystery...' Granny said. 'Mm. Well, there's the death of Marlowe – you remember, from *Shakespeare in Love*. There they go for the official story – that Marlowe and his companions had spent the day at an inn, they were all drunk, a quarrel broke out about the bill, it turned violent, and Marlowe got a dagger in his eye socket. But there are other explanations. It seems likely that Marlowe was employed as a government spy, so he may have been bumped off because he knew too much or was unreliable. The men who were drinking with him on the day he was killed were all employed by the Walsingham family, and Sir Thomas Walsingham was Elizabeth's spymaster – head of MI5!'

Freda considered. 'I think I'd rather write about a woman,' she said.

'Mary Queen of Scots, then? Lots of uncertainties there. Though I must say, I have always thought that she was a silly woman rather than a tragic one.'

'I don't know anything about her really,' Freda said. 'I shall do some research this afternoon and see what I think. I don't have to choose right away. We've got till the end of May to do it.'

'We could watch the two Elizabeth films – Cate Blanchett. They're rather good and they might give you ideas. Maybe we should wait until we can see them on the TV screen. I'm sure Eve would be happy to watch too.'

'How about Colin?'

'If he objects, we can watch in the afternoon, while he's talking to his vegetables.'

'That sounds like a plan,' Freda said, taking her plate and glass over to the dishwasher.

There must have been something a bit unenthusiastic about the way she said it because Granny said, 'We won't just watch educational stuff, I promise. We can all make requests and we're going to need some light relief – so romcoms, old murder mysteries, musicals, reruns of *Harry Potter* if you want. I do want you to have fun and it's hard being with oldies all the time.'

Freda went behind her chair and dropped a kiss on the top of her head. 'You and Eve are quite fun oldies,' she said, 'and us girls do have a blast in the mornings.'

She noticed, as she left the room, that Granny didn't call out to correct *us girls* to *we girls*. 'Your standards are slipping, Granny,' she said to herself as she went up the stairs.

Chapter Five

UNDERLYING ISSUES

April 5th

Freda and I have been declared free of taint and fit company for Eve, and my audit for achievements during our quarantine looks pretty satisfactory: Zoom sessions for my students, *tick*, individual Skype tutorials to discuss dissertations, *tick*, daily walks completed without harm to girls or dogs, *tick*, Colin's vegetables appreciated, *tick*, *The Mirror and the Light* consumed luxuriously, *tick*, quite delicious lemon drizzle cake baked to celebrate our new togetherness, *tick*.

I have also had conversations with David and with Annie. It took me longer than it should have done to get round to this because I felt obscurely guilty that I hadn't suggested spending the lockdown with either of them – my part-time lover or my single daughter – but when I made contact, it was clear that neither of them had thought for a moment of locking down with me.

David, though really fond of me, I think, and true to me in his fashion, said, when I started explaining why I was with Freda and Eve, 'Good choice. I'm glad we know ourselves well enough to realise that locking down together would be the end of us,' and then broke off to answer a call on his work line. And Annie – well, Annie confounded me. She has been in a nine-year relationship, which started when she and

Jon were students and remained provisional all the time he was going through the interminable process of becoming a fully-fledged doctor and she was establishing herself as a barrister in London. Last year, he was offered a consultant's post in Scotland – in Perth, near where he grew up – and he took it. Annie remained in London, which I understood – it's where her work is – and I thought that was the end of them. She went to Perth for Christmas but all the same, I have been steeling myself for things to come to a messy end. Against all expectations, however, she is now in Perth for the duration.

'I'm learning to call it *Pearrth*,' she said, 'and it's rather lovely up here actually. Jon's working terribly hard – cardiologists are much in demand with COVID – so while the courts are closed I'm being a helpmeet – making him meals at the odd times he manages to get home and just generally looking after him.'

This is so unlike Annie that I feel it can't possibly last, but she sounded happy. If this ends in a wedding and a baby, how will I feel about the taming of my difficult, ambitious daughter? I really don't know. The political pundits who bored us to death for months with their speculations on the progress and effects of Brexit have now turned their attention to the pandemic. *We shall all be changed by it* is their mantra. *We shall learn what is really important to us.* Well, I don't want to see Annie changed. We clash often and angrily, but she is clever and fierce and funny and I don't really want to see her dwindle into a wife.

I ring David again this morning. 'So how's crime?' I ask. 'What's COVID doing to it?'

'Have a guess,' he says.

'Well, house-breaking will be down since houses are occupied – and car theft, I imagine, because driving a car draws attention. With the pubs and clubs closed, rapes and assaults will go down – but they'll get moved into homes, with the drinking. Domestic abuse will be rocketing. And there must be clever criminals who are taking advantage – they'll always find an angle. Fake COVID remedies online, and PPE that doesn't work.'

'Pretty much spot on,' he says. 'In the Met, we're watching the drugs scene carefully. They're finding new ways to get the drugs in – cocaine in consignments of face masks and that sort of thing. And the pushers are getting canny. They were driven off the streets but now they're out wearing high-viz vests, looking like key workers. And they're targeting the queues outside the supermarkets.'

'I'm leading a sheltered life up here – food comes to our door. Why are there queues outside supermarkets?'

'A one out, one in rule, and markings on the ground to keep people two metres apart.'

'Good Lord. Are you doing that?'

'You're not going to ask me if I'm eating all right, are you?'

'I am not your mother. But I know your relationship with food shopping – a quick emergency dash just before closing time. I can't imagine you queuing.'

'Click and Collect. Recommended by my neighbour.'

'So she thinks she's your mother?'

'She's a rather attractive young woman.'

'You're lying to me.'

'You'll never know. Live with it.'

As I am closing my phone, I hear the tinkle of a news update coming in. The prime minister has been taken into hospital. The move, we are told, is *precautionary*, but we all saw him looking like death at the Thursday clap for the NHS so it's not looking good. I feel absolutely no goodwill towards him and I am outraged that he has managed to become our prime minister, but the election of a new PM at this juncture would be pretty disastrous, wouldn't it? With Matt Hancock in charge of COVID policy in the meantime. Even I can't make a joke of that.

When I go downstairs I find Eve and Freda in the kitchen discussing Freda's Art project. She has decided on a series of colour-washed sketches of the town square, showing its progression from normal through the changes that have taken place, so she will start with a busy shopping day and then do the emptiness, the rainbows, the blossom coming out on the trees and whatever else is to come. 'I'd like more people, though,' she says. 'People are what I like doing best.'

'How about the Clap for Carers?' I suggest. 'I wonder if anyone goes out to clap there. Some of the shop owners must live above their shops, mustn't they?'

'I could make them up,' Freda says.

'Or we can do research. Next Thursday we'll go along.'

'We're only allowed out once a day.'

'And who's counting? Anyway, we can take Flossie as our cover story.'

'Colin likes to take her for her evening walk.'

'Then we'll all go. He won't mind, will he, Eve?'

'Probably not,' she says, but there is a reservation in her tone. *Back off. Don't try to take over.*

We are actually all getting on very well, and I feel guilty because really this feels like a holiday. We walk Flossie, we talk, Eve and I cook together and we eat well, we drink quite a lot of wine, we watch some great television and some comfortable rubbish and we are all happy, I think, though it is hard to know how Colin is finding it. I was concerned about him having his house full of females but then I remembered that he and Eve brought up four daughters, so he must be used to it. He is perfectly pleasant, praises the food and takes an interest in whatever Freda is doing, but he is a bit remote, and when he is not in the garden he is mainly in his study. I wonder what he does there. When I ask Eve, she looks surprised. 'I don't know. Reads, I suppose,' she says.

The people who really worry me, though, are the

neighbours – the ones with the garden behind ours. I haven't seen the cat for a while but the woman comes out and wanders round the garden, and sometimes I think she might be looking for the cat, and what disturbs me is that the man is often there, just by the door from the house, just watching her. I haven't seen him take her indoors as he did the first time, but it is as though he is monitoring her. When she goes back indoors, he stands aside to let her go in and then he follows, closing the door behind him.

I don't like it, and when Eve and I are making fish pie and baked apples this evening I try a casual enquiry. Looking out into our garden as I am peeling potatoes at the sink, I say, 'When I was a child, our garden backed onto another one like yours does. There was just a hedge between them, and the children who lived there made a hole in it so that we could get into each other's gardens.'

'Sounds like the start of a children's adventure story,' Eve says.

'Idealised in memory, no doubt,' I say. 'Your neighbours don't have children, do they? I haven't seen any playing out there.'

'No,' she says. 'No, they don't. They've not been married long, I think.'

'Do you know them well?'

'Not particularly, no.'

She seems to be shutting down the conversation, but I say, 'She seems to be fond of the cat.'

'Mm,' she says, concentrating on coring the apples.

'But he's not so keen,' I say.

'Mm,' she says again. 'Raisins or sultanas in these?'

'What? Oh, raisins.'

There is a pause, and then she says, 'Paul's a plumber – our neighbour. He put our en suite in for us.'

And I have a distinct sense that this piece of information

has been dolloped out to me to stop me from making any further enquiries. Too bad. 'And what does she do?' I ask.

There is a very long silence while Eve makes a business of stuffing raisins into the apples and I think she may not be going to answer, but she takes the dish of apples over to the oven, puts it in and turns to look at me. 'Elise? She's a teaching assistant and she's a bit fragile,' she says, and she switches the radio on for the evening news.

We mend our rift, if there has been one, over an evening spent watching *Elizabeth, The Virgin Queen*, the excuse for watching it being that Freda might find an idea for her project. Colin opts out and retires to his study with the rest of the second bottle of wine that we opened at supper time.

'Your choice tomorrow,' Eve tells him.

'Fine,' he says. 'I'm sure some channel is showing *Greatest Rugby Matches of All Time*.'

It is a pretty girly evening. We eat fudge, comment on the hair and dresses and join in Freda's outrage at the way the men all try to tell the new queen what to do. Freda takes a particular dislike to William Cecil, played by the elderly Richard Attenborough. At the point where he tells the queen's ladies-in-waiting that he wants to inspect her bedsheets every morning, Freda buries her face in her hands and says, 'That is so disgusting!'

'I think that was probably the case with all queens,' I say. 'Their bodies were public property. Their only function really was to produce heirs. These men can't get their heads round the idea that Elizabeth's function is actually to rule the country.'

'Well, he's an old creep,' she says.

'He can't actually have been as old as that when she came to the throne,' I say, 'because he went on being her chief minister for years. He was probably only about forty.'

'Even creepier,' she says, and takes another piece of fudge.

Chapter Six

STAY AT HOME

April 9th

So the prime minister wasn't actually going to die. This had been so weird. When he was first ill, it felt like a joke – he was so useless he couldn't even stop himself from catching COVID, let alone anyone else – but then it was real and scary. It was even a bit of a downer on their morning singing; it didn't feel right to be too upbeat and jolly.

So she was glad that he seemed to be recovering, because in other ways life was really good – so good she had to feel guilty about it when people were dying. The most exciting thing was that she was going to be in the YouTube video that Grace and her friends were making. A friend of Grace's from her performing arts school was making the video. They would each record their part on their phones, and then he would put it all together. It sounded crazy but she had seen other things on YouTube that must have been done like that, so it had to be possible. She was still practising and she hadn't dared to record anything yet, but she had promised Grace she would do it by the weekend.

The other good thing was that she had found the subject for her history project and she was really excited about it. The idea had started from watching *Elizabeth*, as Granny thought it would, and it started from a puzzle, which was what she was looking for. When it looked as though the queen might marry Lord Robert Dudley, who she was in love with, there was the surprise moment when creepy old Cecil shouted, 'You can't marry him. He's married already.' And then the queen was furious and banished Lord Robert from court. But Freda couldn't see why on earth he would have secretly married someone else when there was a chance that he might marry the queen. So she had googled him and found that Granny had been quite right about the way people twist the truth in history. Robert Dudley's marriage to Amy Robsart wasn't secret at all. They had been married for eight years by the time Elizabeth became queen and Lord Robert became her favourite, and they had been married in a royal palace at a ceremony attended by King Edward VI himself. The film was simply lying! It was true that Robert and Amy were both a few days under eighteen when they married, and that it was not an arranged marriage. William Cecil, who was a guest at the wedding, called it a *carnal marriage* and Freda had looked up what that meant. It meant that it was all about sex, and of course pervy Cecil would have been interested in that. You might think that Amy's father, who was a rich landowner but not an aristocrat, would have been happy for his daughter to marry the son of the Duke of Northumberland, one of the most powerful men in the country, but the duke might not have been so pleased. Wikipedia (and she knew you couldn't necessarily trust that) said that he was pleased to strengthen his influence in Norfolk, where the Robsarts lived, and as soon as he was married, Robert became a Member of Parliament for Norfolk, so that made some sense. What didn't make sense to Freda was that neither set of parents gave the couple any money. Amy was her father's only child and his heir, but she didn't have a dowry, and she and Robert didn't have a proper home and lived mainly on handouts from Robert's father. Maybe Amy's father didn't trust Robert with the money. Maybe he hadn't been so keen on the marriage. When Cecil said it was *carnal*, could that mean that Amy was pregnant? If so, she lost the baby because she and Robert didn't have any children.

What she found when she did some more searching was that there was quite a famous mystery about how Amy died, because just when the rumours about the queen marrying Lord Robert were at their strongest, Amy apparently fell down some stairs in the dark when she was alone in someone else's house, and broke her neck. Officially it was an accident. Unofficially, suicide and murder were suspected. So this was her real mystery, but to Freda's mind there were others too, and they were all linked to one another. She wrote them down:

1. If the marriage was all about sex, why didn't Robert and Amy have any children?
2. If everyone knew Robert was married, how did they think he was going to marry the queen?
3. How and why did Amy die?
4. Why did the queen not marry Robert after Amy's death?

Four good questions. She didn't kid herself that she was going to find The Truth, because, as she was learning, there was apparently no such thing with history, but she could come up with some good theories. She knew Granny would love to get involved, but this was her project and she was keeping it to herself.

That evening after supper they went into the town square to see what the Clap for Carers looked like there. Freda had been given the job of asking Colin if they could make that Flossie's evening walk and he had been nice about it, though he couldn't be persuaded that it was all right for Eve to come too.

'That's not shielding,' he said. 'You know you're not supposed to go outside the house. Be sensible, Eve.'

'I go outside the house to clap for carers normally, don't I?' she argued. 'What difference does it make if I walk down the road a bit?'

'And when you're walking down the road a bit and someone comes running up to say hello, what happens then?'

She gave in, but Freda felt sorry for her as they left, and was sorry that she wouldn't be able to discuss her drawing with her.

'Take photos,' Eve called as they left.

The square actually took her breath away. It was dark, except for the street lamps in each corner, but nearly every shop had lights in its windows, and in the windows above, candles and lamps that glowed among the shadows. Hastily she got her phone out and started taking photos. It was going to be a huge challenge to get that effect on paper. She would have to ask Eve how she could get the effect of those pools of light. There came into her mind an image of one of Nico's favourite books – a Christmas book – where the houses were all night-time black, with yellow windows scattered about. That wasn't the effect she wanted at all. She wanted to get the grades of black and grey, and the way the lights flickered and their glow faded away at the edges. It was exciting and scary thinking about trying to get it right and probably messing up totally.

There were quite a few people standing about for the clapping, and some people had whistles to blow and saucepan lids to bang. Colin was muttering that it was all very fine but what NHS staff needed was proper protective equipment, but he did clap, looping Flossie's lead over his arm. She barked when the noise started but she seemed to be more excited than frightened, and when it was finished Colin picked her up and Freda liked the look on his face as he gave her a cuddle.

They waved farewells (it was like New Year's Eve, Freda thought, when everyone was suddenly friendly with people they didn't know) and then they walked back home along a street that seemed dark and lonely after the lights and noise in the square. She felt comfortable, though, enclosed in this little circle – Granny, Colin, Flossie – just as she would have been with Mum and Ben and Nico, and it made her think about Amy Robsart/Dudley and the dark lonely night when she died.

'What happened to you?' she whispered. 'What really happened?'

Chapter Seven

TESTING MY EYESIGHT

April 19ᵗʰ

We have been here for a month now and though we have a *modus vivendi* with which we all seem to be happy, there is a whiff of tension in the air. It is mainly around Colin, and we can all see that this is the most difficult for him. I have wondered from the start why Eve felt the need to fill the house, and Colin must wonder this too, surely. I think she was genuinely thinking about me stuck on my own in a comatose London, but it must have been too that she didn't welcome the idea of being alone with Colin for months on end. If Colin suspects that she was afraid of being bored, that must be hurtful, mustn't it? And there is an undeniably female atmosphere in the house; Colin must hear the gales of laughter sometimes from the kitchen, and though we have been scrupulous about taking turns in choosing the TV-watching, and have sat without complaint through *The Magnificent Seven* and *A Bridge Too Far*, plus several documentaries that would not have been my choice, he often retreats to his study in the evenings. And he is drinking too much. We joked at first about how good lockdown was going to be for the wine business, and I am the first to welcome a glass with dinner, and a bottle between the three of us would be just fine, but what Colin does is find that we really need to open a second bottle just to top up our glasses, and then to take the rest of it away with him. And the bottle of whiskey I brought disappeared long ago. And drinking doesn't cheer him up – it just makes him gloomier, it seems to me. But he is always nice to Freda, I must say, and she goes to him with questions, which I'm glad about because it makes him feel a part of things, but which riles me too, because I like to be the person Freda asks, and here she is, constantly consulting Eve about her Art work and asking Colin about God knows what, and refusing even to tell me what her History project is about, even though I have given her all sorts of helpful pointers and feel myself to be an expert on Elizabethan England at the moment, now I've finished *Hamnet*. So, as you can see, I am ratty too, but I have decreed that we are all watching *Hamlet* tonight – the black cast version streamed from the RSC – and I shall be the undeniable expert.

It is Sunday, so for lunch Eve and I cook a roast chicken with lemon sauce, with a lot of roast potatoes and Colin's purple sprouting, broccoli and then we stuff ourselves with rhubarb crumble and ice cream. After that, once we have stacked the dishwasher, what I really feel like doing is slobbing in front of the television watching something undemanding, but Freda puts me to shame by saying she has work to get on with, so I go upstairs with her, leaving Eve and Colin to have some time together.

I take a look at the introductory sections of dissertations that three students have sent to me for comment. It is a difficult business being the language consultant on these dissertations. I don't meddle with content – they are writing on subjects about which I know nothing, anyway – and it's not up to me to comment on structure either. All I am supposed to do is give guidance where language problems get in the way of comprehensibility. I can point out straightforward grammatical/lexical errors, but the problem is that quite often when the language goes off the rails, it means that the thought processes have derailed too. The syntax is a muddle because the argument is a muddle but it's not my brief to rewrite anything, so I have to nudge them into clarifying their thoughts, and that's a taxing thing to be doing on a Sunday afternoon when you have overdone the carbs.

So this may be the reason why I find myself gazing out of the window and noticing the man in his garden. Usually I see the wife down at the bottom of the garden – sometimes with the cat, though I haven't seen it recently – and the husband stands up by the house, watching her. This afternoon, though, there is no sign of her, and he is at the end of the garden, apparently taking an interest in our apple trees, now in blossom, and smoking a cigarette. I haven't seen him with a cigarette before – except I have. I am certain, as I watch, that he is the man who lurks under the trees by the lake in the mornings. The stance is right – broad shoulders and a slightly hunched, tense way of holding himself – but it's the way he smokes that makes me see him now as the same man. I was a smoker myself once and gave it up thirteen years ago for Freda's sake. Cigarettes were my friends and I drew on them lovingly, as most smokers do. This man smokes in short, hard drags, as though he hates the thing in his hand, and so does the man by the lake. From the window I can't see his face clearly, and up till yesterday I had not really seen the face of the man by the lake, since he always had his hood up, but the weather has improved and he had the hood down yesterday, so I had a chance to look at him properly. I would recognise him if I could get closer.

Abandoning my dissertations, I speed downstairs and out into the garden. Once outside, I make myself slow down; I am visible from the sitting room, where Eve and Colin are. I do my best to stroll idly down the garden, though there is a light drizzle going on, so it's not the obvious time for a stroll.

I pause once or twice to look at a shrub or two, and then I go on to the kitchen garden and the fruit trees at the end.

The man is still there, so I drop to my knees and take a keen interest in the asparagus patch. From here I venture a look to the garden beyond. Damn! He has his back to me now. Is he about to head back to the house? I watch, willing him to turn, and he does. He turns just for a moment, to throw his cigarette end into the weedy patch under the fence, but it is enough. It is the same man. Vindicated, I jump up as soon as he starts back towards the house, and turn – to bump straight into Eve.

I say the most stupid thing possible under the circumstances. 'Why are you spying on me?' I ask.

She laughs. 'Me, spying?' she says, and gives me that look she used to give the kids at school, as though she knows exactly what I'm up to and she is not going to judge me, but she would like to help me to do better. Then she turns to go back to the house. 'You've ruined your trousers, do you know that?' she says.

I scamper along to catch up with her. 'I was just checking the asparagus,' I say with all the conviction I can muster. 'Don't you love the first asparagus of the year?'

There is a long pause before she answers. 'Well, I do. But I know better than to interfere with the vegetables. We'll leave them to the expert, shall we?'

I go back upstairs as soon as we are back in the house. I am thoroughly humiliated – not so much at being caught among the vegetables spying on the neighbours as by my pathetic pretence. Why didn't I just tell her the truth? I'm sure her pupils felt just the same, when *My little brother tore it up*, *Somebody must have taken it* and *I left it on the bus* were greeted with that same clear-eyed, tolerant scepticism. In my case, the truth is not that shameful, after all. The man behaves oddly and there is some reason to be concerned for his wife. My need to check whether the odd man who loiters to watch our morning walk is the same man who loiters at his back door watching his wife when she is in the garden is not unreasonable, is it? There is nothing prurient about it. But I was warned off. Eve doesn't want me to get interested in her neighbours and she made it clear. As a guest in her house, I have behaved badly, and then lied ineptly. Chagrin makes me hot with discomfort and all I can do is hide.

When we convene in the evening for *Hamlet*, Eve is her usual self, and with no hint of lingering reproach she suggests a cheese and biscuits supper after our hefty lunch, to be eaten while watching the play, and the two of us assemble the supper on the coffee table before calling Freda and Colin to join us. I know there is a danger that I will try to save my *amour propre* by giving a learned commentary to the play, so I resolve to be a model of all patience and just let them get on with it – unless anyone asks a question, of course.

It is a riveting production of the play, with an outstanding performance by Paapa Essiedu as Hamlet. There is a simple concept: Denmark simply becomes an African country. At the opening, without any non-Shakespearean text written in, we see the young black prince – Hamlet, Prince of Denmark – called up by name to receive his degree from the University of Wittenberg. And then we move to Africa and the play begins. The only white faces we see are those of his old university friends – the Europeans, Rosencrantz and Guildenstern – come to visit him from Wittenberg. Once she gets her head round the idea of Denmark being in Africa, Freda loves it. She is sitting beside me on the sofa, and I can feel her responses – to the ghost, to Hamlet's mania, to the savage humour and the vivid colours of set and costume.

I, meanwhile, reflect as I always do on just how badly the women get treated. There are only the two of them – Hamlet's mother, Gertrude, newly married to Hamlet's uncle Claudius, his father's murderer, now Denmark's king; and the woman Hamlet loves, Ophelia, the daughter of Polonius, the new king's chief minister. Routinely these days, directors try to address the gender imbalance by casting a woman as either Rosencrantz or Guildenstern, and one of the ambassadors returned from Norway is often female too, but it is a very male play. Three sons looking to avenge their fathers drive the plot along. They judge themselves and their honour as men by their will to avenge, and they judge the women's honour by their chastity and its perceived breaches. I don't think I am imagining Freda's discomfort at the relentless questioning and badgering of Ophelia about her sex life. They are all obsessed with her chastity: Laertes, her brother, heading off for student life in Paris, warns her off letting Hamlet get too close; Polonius, her father, a man who spies on her conversation with her lover and hides himself in the queen's private chamber, tells her that Hamlet can't possibly love her and is only after sex; Hamlet, her lover, first showers her with gifts and declarations of love and then yells at her to get herself to a nunnery. No wonder she goes mad, and no wonder when she loses her mind that she sings about sex. I liked a recent production I saw in which Ophelia's drowning was no accident; the king's henchmen simply disposed of her. Used by Hamlet, by her father, by the king, she was disposed of when she became an inconvenience.

Well, that's the lecture I would have given if anyone had asked me, but nobody did, and those who have heard me binding on about this sort of stuff before may think that's a good thing. As it is, I have made a mental note to tell Freda about Polonius and William Cecil, because I think she will like that.

I get my opportunity sooner than I expected. We take a break at interval time and Colin offers to make tea. He goes off to the kitchen and Eve gathers up our supper debris and goes out to join him. I think I can hear her emptying the dishwasher.

'You know William Cecil, who you took such a dislike to in the film the other night?' I say.

'Pervy old man inspecting the queen's bedsheets? Yes.'

'Well, he wasn't actually as old as the film makes him, but he was old by the time he died and he had been the queen's chief minister for years, and the public would have felt that they knew him. He died the year before Shakespeare wrote Hamlet, and there is a suggestion in some quarters that Shakespeare based the character of Polonius on him. He couldn't be accused of slander because Cecil was dead.'

'Sounds about right,' Freda says. 'Polonius would have inspected the queen's sheets, given half a chance. Hiding in her bedroom! He deserved stabbing!' She is quiet for a moment, and then she asks, 'Is there actually any evidence that Shakespeare was writing about him?'

'It's a bit circumstantial, but he did publish a letter he wrote to his son, giving him precepts for life, in the same way that Polonius gives his precepts to his son. I have read Cecil's precepts, and some of his advice is similar to Polonius's in principle – how to choose friends wisely, not to be a borrower or a lender – but quite a lot of it is different, and the language is different of course, because Polonius is speaking in verse and Cecil is even more long-winded than he is. But I suppose the fact that people knew Cecil had written his ten precepts might have made them see Polonius's precepts as similar.'

'Or perhaps it's just what those pompous old men were like,' Freda says, and Colin comes in with the tea.

Later, as I am thinking myself into sleep, I remember that I should have told Freda about Katharine Hamlet, a young woman who drowned in the river Avon, just outside Stratford, when Shakespeare was fifteen. The coroner's judgement was that she slipped and drowned by accident, but local talk was that she was heartbroken over a love affair. *Did she go to the water or did the water come to her?* I wonder as I drop off to sleep.

Chapter Eight

VIRAL LOAD

April 22nd

Detective Superintendent David Scott cursed quietly to himself as he walked at speed back to his office and hoped sincerely that Gina Gray would not get to see his virtual press conference. As he slammed the door closed behind him, his inner ear conjured up her voice, needling and sardonic. *It's not as though I'm setting the bar that high, David. I'm not asking for polished rhetoric, just eschewing the most obvious of clichés is all I hope for.*

Well, it wasn't as easy as all that. He sat down at his desk and put his head in his hands. The statement to the press was easy enough – you could craft that beforehand. It was the questions that tripped you up; find yourself wrong-footed and the clichés just rolled off the tongue: *This very difficult time, Number one priority, No stone unturned, Pursuing every possible lead.* He had at least avoided *unprecedented circumstances.* He was not a violent or vindictive man, but he thought he would quite like to see any politician or journalist who used the word *unprecedented* in the next three months put in the stocks to have rotten cabbages thrown at them. He would quite like to hear Gina on that subject. He hadn't talked to her recently, but she would have a view – particularly about *very unprecedented* or *more unprecedented*. He could hear her, as he had heard her go on about *very unique* and *more original. Unprecedented is not a gradable adjective. It is binary. Things either have a precedent or they don't.*

He jumped up and walked to the window. This was just distraction. The clichés in his press conference were not what was making him sick at heart. This sickness he knew of old, and it came from a knowledge deep inside him that there was nothing he or his colleagues could do. Rebecca Clarke, aged seventeen, junior prefect, star of the school athletics team and possessor of a Duke of Edinburgh's gold award, clever, pretty, popular, and the darling of her parents' hearts, was not going to be found alive, whatever resources they put into looking for her. It was forty-eight hours now since she had been reported missing after failing to come back from her morning jog along the River Mole in her upmarket suburb on the London/Surrey border. Every instinct told him that she had been dead all that time.

You got to feel it after a while in the job, and the press hacks knew it too. They didn't give front page space to every teenage girl who disappeared. They smelt a tragedy here. They probably knew the statistics as well as he did: getting on for 13,000 under-eighteens were reported missing in the UK every year on average. Roughly thirty-eight a day – more than one an hour. Some of those would turn up soon with tales of missed buses, uncharged phones and losing track of the time. Others had been driven from home by abuse and neglect, and others still had been lured away by predators and traffickers. And sometimes they had been murdered.

In the past forty-eight hours, his colleagues had interviewed Rebecca's parents, teachers and friends; they had combed through her bedroom, examining her clothes, the drawers of her desk, the contents of her waste paper basket. They had taken her computer away and trawled her emails, her Facebook contacts, her Tweets, her online searches.

Her phone was missing with her and as silent as she was. There was nothing, not even the slightest hint, to suggest that anything could have made her disappear from choice. She was successful at school, cheerful at home. She had had a boyfriend for a while last year but he had gone to a sixth form college to do his A-levels and they had parted amicably. These days she socialised happily with her girl friends. The friends said that plenty of boys fancied her but she wanted to focus on her athletics and her A-levels. Everywhere the investigating team looked in her life, they could find only security, happiness and hope. She had not gone missing; someone had killed her.

His phone rang. He looked at the caller ID and was tempted to let it ring out, but she was persistent. He would have to talk to her some time.

'Gina,' he said.

'David.'

'What can I do for you?'

'I'm very well, thank you. How are you?'

'I'm fine, but you only call when you want something, so what is it?'

'Are you looking for Becky Clarke?'

'Well, I'm not the SIO because I'm a superintendent and the clue's in the name, and I'm not driving around in a car looking for her because no police officer does that in the real world.'

'But you are in charge of the case?'

'I have a watching brief. And she is called Rebecca. Her parents call her Rebecca, and so do her friends. The press have decided to call her Becky because they think it makes us feel that we all know her.'

'You're upset. You don't think you're going to find her, do you?'

'I am not *upset*. I am concerned, as we all are. And I'm not speculating on —'

'You're *upset*. I know when you're upset. You get angry. Because you think being angry is more manly than being upset.'

'Is there actually any point in this conversation, Gina? Because if not, I do have a few things to do.'

'I'd like to help.'

He laughed, though not terribly convincingly, he had to admit. 'From Cumbria you're going to find our misper for us?'

'I understand young people. I'm a teacher. Given some information, I may be able to —'

'Any information that we think it would be useful for the public to have is available in the media. Watch the evening news. You'll probably see an extract from my press conference. And I don't need a review of my performance, thank you. This one isn't for you, Gina. Don't get invested in it.'

He rang off and stood staring at his phone for a moment before he put it away. Would Gina have seen something his team had missed? Something in the language of Rebecca Clarke's social media exchanges? Something that suggested that she had secrets after all? Secrets that made it possible that she was still alive?

He shook off the idea. Gina was clever but she couldn't work magic. He was as certain as he could be that Rebecca Clarke had not chosen to go missing, in her jogging gear, without spare clothes or a toothbrush, with nothing but the phone in her pocket.

He looked at the pile of print-offs that had been left on his desk – press coverage of the story so far. There was a moral panic brewing, he could see, about the emptiness of streets and footpaths during the lockdown, the absence of *bobbies on the beat*, a putative rise in assaults, especially on young women. He knew that assaults outside the home had dropped dramatically, in fact, but when did the media let facts get in the way of a good panic? The *Guardian*, he noticed, always looking for a promising limb to go out on, was raising the issue of mental health in the young – the anxiety about missed schooling and exams, the isolation from friends, the tensions of family life, the extra volume of social media traffic. *Could stress have driven Rebecca to leave home?* it asked. *If only*, he thought.

His SIO's best guess was that she was in the river. There was a scuffed patch on the river bank where a body could have been dragged. The forensic team was doing a microscopic search. Whether or not they found anything to link to Rebecca, if her body wasn't found in twenty-four hours, he would have the river dragged. He could at least give her parents certainty. People always said that it was the not knowing that was the hardest thing. He wasn't sure. He thought that knowing would be the worst.

Chapter Nine

SOCIAL DISTANCE

April 23rd

As she hung up Flossie's lead and went to wash her hands, Freda admitted to herself that the mornings were not quite as much fun as they had been at the start. Now they had done the YouTube video and it had been good and they had had plenty of likes on Facebook, but it hadn't gone viral like they had secretly hoped, and they had no excuse for singing on their walks anymore, and anyway, people had started to get tired of the singing and had drifted away. Even that woman in the red tracksuit wasn't out when they were out anymore. And she hadn't seen that man who watched from under the trees for a few days. Not that that was a bad thing. He gave her the creeps.

So, all in all, the morning walk wasn't quite as special as it had been, though it was still fun, and Grace and Venetia had decided that they each had to tell three jokes every morning – and that included Granny, who was still coming out with them every morning – and the weather was getting better, and the lake was beautiful, and Flossie enjoyed herself, so there was nothing to grumble about really. And anyway, the rest of the day was more interesting now that she had her History project to work on. In her internet searches on Amy Robsart, she had found a book about her that looked really good and

Eve, who understood why she didn't want to involve her grandmother, had ordered it for her online. It had arrived that morning and she couldn't wait to get into it, but first she had promised to do baking with Granny – a birthday cake for Shakespeare, made with the ingredients from a shopping list in one of his plays. It was one of Granny's nutty ideas but a cake was never a bad thing.

Although she wasn't letting Granny in on the project, she had unknowingly said some helpful things when they watched *Hamlet* the other night. There was Polonius and Cecil, but also, the next day, she had told her about Katharine Hamlet drowning in the river and the coroner's verdict of suicide, but her friends' opinion that she was heartbroken and might have drowned herself. The gravediggers in the play think Ophelia might have drowned herself from grief, though the coroner said it was an accident. What Freda could see was that coroners didn't know much in those days because the forensic evidence was pretty basic – nothing like you saw in TV crime dramas now. All the coroner could say about Amy was that she was alone, the stairs were steep and she fell all the way to the bottom, that she had two head wounds and a broken neck and would have died instantly. Accident, suicide or murder? Who could tell?

It made her think about Becky Clarke. Facebook and Twitter were full of everyone's theories about what had happened to her but nobody knew anything really, except that she had gone missing while she was out jogging. People said she was being stalked by someone at school, or that she was stressed about missing school, or that she was upset about splitting up with her boyfriend, but they weren't people who knew her, were they? It was like everyone was seeing themselves in her place and putting their own problems on her.

The fruit cake was made and it smelt delicious as it was cooking, ginger and nutmeg and caramelising sugar floating up the stairs to where she sat poring over her new book's account of Robert and Amy Dudley's marriage. The author, Christine Hartweg, didn't make much of the fact that they had no children – she just said that a surprisingly large number of marriages were childless in the sixteenth century – but Freda thought that it was another thing that helped to give the impression that theirs wasn't really a proper marriage. It was like her always being called 'Amy Robsart' in accounts of her life. Why never Amy Dudley? The coroner called her 'Lady Amy Dudley', quite correctly, so why did no-one else? So she wanted to know about why there were no children. Robert Dudley had a son with his second wife, so the problem must have been Amy's. Freda's mum had a friend who was trying to get pregnant and doing IVF, and it was all quite a drama, but she was quite old – nearly forty, she thought, and Mum said that was the problem; she had left it too late. But Amy hadn't left it too late. Freda decided she would pluck up courage and ask Colin about it. It couldn't be that embarrassing, could it, not when he had been a doctor for years?

They ate the birthday cake for tea. It was nicely spicy and full of fruit but a bit solid and could only be eaten in small helpings. It was going to take them a while to finish it. Granny said fruit cakes lasted forever, but did they want to be eating it forever?

After tea seemed to be the moment to catch Colin. He had finished working in the garden and was flicking through the Radio Times, so she asked if he had a moment for a medical question. It was the wrong approach, it turned out, because he thought she was feeling ill and started to explain that he couldn't treat her as her doctor, but once they had sorted that out, he was really helpful. She didn't understand everything he said because he used some medical terms she didn't know, but she got the basic gist, and now she knew that:

If Amy was not able to conceive, there were several possible causes to do with ovulation and hormones.

If she conceived but had miscarriages, one of the most likely reasons was an 'incompetent cervix'. (How horrible to be told you had an *incompetent* cervix – it made it sound as though it was definitely your fault.)

She had asked him what she feared was a dumb question – about whether Amy not being able to have children could be connected with the *malady of the breast* that she was rumoured to have when she died – and he didn't seem to think it was dumb. He said the breast malady probably meant cancer, and there had been several studies to see if frequent miscarriages predisposed women to breast cancer, but the results showed that they didn't.

'So it looks as though your Amy was just very unlucky,' he said.

So, maybe in the end that was what you had to say about her: she was unlucky in marrying a man who could only succeed in the world if he separated himself from her, unlucky in being *barren* (that was the word they used), unlucky in getting cancer, and unlucky in falling downstairs. Perhaps none of them were connected. Perhaps she was just a person that bad things happened to.

She went upstairs, made some notes, and then rang her mum, who sounded a bit fraught. When she mentioned the Shakespeare cake, Mum said, 'Oh, for the chance to bake a cake. Everyone's doing lockdown baking and I'd love to make a cake with Nico, but Nonna won't let me into my own kitchen. She's in there all the time. The food is lovely but I want to cook!'

'Have you told her?'

'She just says, *Oh, you have your work to do*. But I don't – it's school holidays. What I'm doing is endlessly trying to keep Nico amused.'

'Can't Ben help?'

'He's got some music project he's doing, and when he's not doing that, Nonno's got him out in the garden working on his vegetables.'

'Would it be easier if I was there?'

Her mother considered. 'I don't think so. I miss you, of course, but I think you'd be fed up and I'd have you to worry about too. You sound as though you're having a good time.'

'I am. I've got two excellent projects to work on. I'll tell you more when I've made more progress.'

'Is Granny helping?'

'Eve has helped a bit with the Art project, but I'm not letting Granny anywhere near the other one. She means well, but you know…'

'I do know. What a wise girl you are.'

Feeling a bit desolate after she rang off, Freda went downstairs, where she found her grandmother sitting at the kitchen table in floods of tears, with Eve beside her, passing her pieces of kitchen paper to mop up with. She didn't think she had ever seen Granny cry before and it was a thoroughly unsettling sight. It flashed through her mind that nothing could be wrong down in Marlbury because she had just been talking to her mum, so something must be wrong with Auntie Annie.

'What's happened?' she asked.

Eve said, 'It's all right, my love. Did you hear? They've found a body near where Becky Clarke disappeared. They haven't said it's definitely her yet, but it's likely, and your granny's a bit upset.'

'I'm not upset!' Granny blurted from behind a wodge of kitchen paper. 'I'm furious. These bloody men on the loose think they can just use girls and chuck them away – and everyone just accepts it as a fact of life and –'

'Come on now, darling,' Eve said. 'We don't accept it.

There'll be a huge manhunt for this guy, and they nearly always get them in the end, don't they?'

'David knew she was dead,' Granny said. 'They all knew.'

'The police must hate these cases. Think what it must do to them.'

'Don't tell me I've got to feel sorry for the police! What about her mother? That poor, poor woman.'

And she was off into tears again.

Eve stood up and went to put an arm round Freda and lead her out into the hall. 'She'll be all right,' she whispered. 'She hates not being able to do anything. She'd like to be down there, finding the man who did this.'

'Well, she couldn't, could she?' Freda said. 'I mean, even if there wasn't lockdown. It's nothing to do with her, is it?'

'That's not what she thinks,' Eve said.

Chapter Ten

FOLLOW THE SCIENCE

April 24th

'Are you really doing anything? Is there any chance that you're going to catch this bastard or are you just going through the motions? Because I think I could—'

'Gina, just stop. Listen to yourself. Yes, we are doing things. I have a strong team working on this and I'm about to go and talk to them now, and I can get on with the job faster if I'm not interrupted by crazy women phoning me.'

'But what have you got? Have you got her phone? Her emails? You know I've helped before. Language insights. You could use me as an expert. If I could see them I'm sure I would be able to—'

'We have experts – of course we do. You sound a bit unhinged, frankly. I think lockdown is getting to you. Just because you've been able to muscle in on a few cases and you've struck lucky with your language stuff doesn't mean you can get involved any time you like. There's nothing you can offer here. You're not here, you didn't know Rebecca Clarke and you're wasting my time.'

'I know seventeen-year-old girls. I taught them for years.'

'We're talking to her teachers. They know her. Now I'm going. And I'm not talking about this again.'

'Are you going to do another press conference?'

'Probably.'

'Well, try to say something meaningful this time, is my advice.'

He rang off.

The meeting room where the team was gathered felt odd. It was a large room, chosen for keeping a distance, and perhaps it was the fact that the officers were spread out rather than huddled together that seemed to have drained the energy from the room. It was a dull morning and the fluorescent lights were on, pasting them all with a pallid sheen. They stood up as he came in but the faces they turned to him were unwilling and dull-eyed. What had they thought was going to happen? Hadn't they all known that this was how it would end? That the previous days had been the prelude to tracking down a murderer?

He cursed Gina. Tangling with her meant he hadn't composed his message to the troops with inspiration in mind. Willing energy into his body language, he strode to the front of the room.

'We're all disappointed,' he said, 'and I can see that's how you're feeling, but I hope you're angry, too. We take seriously every life ended by violence, but when we see a young woman with so much promise in her life senselessly killed, we can't help taking it personally. We're trained to be objective, to keep our personal feelings in check, but we are all human. If you feel angry, use the energy from that anger and bring the man who did this to justice. There is nothing we can do to help Rebecca's parents in their grief, but we can give them justice. DCI Ireland will brief you in detail now about preliminary forensics. One piece of good luck is that it looks as though we will be able to retrieve information from Rebecca's phone. But what I do want to impress on you – and I can't emphasise this enough – is that we must have absolute confidentiality in this case. You're all aware that there is intense media interest. This type of case always attracts interest, but the lockdown means that people have time on their hands and, frankly, they are hungry for news about something other than COVID-19. Reporters will use every trick in the book to get information out of you. If I find that any information has been leaked, I shall come down very hard on the culprits. There must be no leaks.'

Every trick in the book? he thought as he returned to his office. Still, he hadn't said *unprecedented*, had he?

At the end of the day – a day that had included an attempt at a meaningful press statement and an exchange with a bad-tempered assistant commissioner, hungry for crumbs to throw to the media – there was a knock at his door, and DCI Tom Ireland came into his office. He was a big man with a deceptively slow style of speech, but Scott had learnt not to underestimate him. He was shrewd and he was determined. Scott thought he was probably pretty ruthless too. This evening he had an unmistakeable air of achievement.

'News for me, Tom?' he asked.

'Yes. Though we're still trying to process it. The autopsy report… you might like to see. She was strangled, as we could see. From behind. Someone threw a ligature over her head from behind – probably a piece of electric flex. She wasn't raped. No sign of sexual assault at all. No signs of a struggle. It looks almost like a contract killing – planned, quick, efficient.'

'That's very odd, isn't it? As though someone wanted to silence her?'

'The phone has given us something. Two text messages.'

'She'd arranged to meet someone?'

'Rather the opposite. These are the messages.'

Scott scanned the sheet of paper he was handed. 'So, one sent the day before she went missing, and the other on the day. You've traced the owner of the phone?'

'We have. Joshua Clements, aged sixteen, fellow pupil at Greenacres High School, in the year below Rebecca.'

'You've talked to him?'

'Yes.'

'What's he got to say for himself?'

He watched Tom Ireland hesitate. 'He's not very bright – well, you can see from the texts he's no great shakes academically. He's in the remedial classes at school. *Compensatory*, they call them there. We've talked to his mother. Sensible sort of woman – runs a dress shop in the local high street. Divorced, nice home, the boy is her only child. She and Andrea Clarke – Rebecca's mother – are friends. She says Joshua has always struggled at school but he's good at practical subjects. He's never been in trouble and never violent. And she gives him an alibi. Says he is never good at getting up in the morning and she has to badger him to get up. She went into his room and woke him after nine that morning. Rebecca Clarke went out for her run at seven thirty.'

'But you've only got her word for that? Does the school confirm that the boy isn't violent?'

'I've got an appointment to see the deputy head tomorrow morning. There's the matter of the phone to sort out too.'

'Does he deny the phone's his?'

'No. He agrees that it's his number, but he says he hasn't got the phone. He had it confiscated the day before lockdown and didn't get it back before the school closed.'

'And what does the school say?'

'That all phones were returned to pupils on the last day before lockdown. They have a strict policy about phones in class. Anyone who has a phone out has it confiscated, and it's locked in the safe in the office next to the headmaster's room, in a labelled envelope. At the end of the day, they can go to pick it up, and they sign for it.'

'And Joshua Clements signed for his?'

'Apparently. That's what we need to check tomorrow.'

'And where are you with the boy?'

'We talked to him at home. It was… difficult. He seemed to be genuinely upset about Rebecca's death. His mother says he and Rebecca used to play together when they were little and she was always nice to him, even though she was *in the smart set.*'

'You would think messages like this would have upset her. But her parents didn't notice anything about her mood that day?'

'We haven't talked to them again since the body was found. The family liaison officer has been with them, of course, but we haven't interviewed them again. I'd like to leave it for a day or two.'

'What was the boy's attitude? How did he seem?'

'Well, that's the thing. I don't think he's bright enough to be a good actor and he seemed genuinely bewildered.'

'What's he like physically?'

'He's a big lad. Strong enough to strangle her and get her into the river.'

'Have you ever read *Of Mice and Men?*'

'It was one of our GCSE books.'

'For me too. Perhaps it's permanently on the syllabus. But the way you talk about Joshua Clements makes me think of Lennie.'

'Who kills the girl, doesn't he?'

'He does. You'll find out more about Joshua? Talk to his teachers. Talk to Rebecca's friends again, find out if he was pestering her. And, unless you get any lead on who else might have his phone, you're going to have to bring him in for a formal interview, aren't you?'

'He's been told that's going to happen.'

'Good. I'd like to watch that, Tom. I don't want to be

breathing down your neck and I've got every faith in you to handle this sensitively, but the public mood and the media are so volatile at the moment. We've got a murder victim who looks like everyone's ideal daughter and our potential suspect is a boy with learning difficulties. It could blow up in our faces very easily, and I'll be the one to carry the can.'

He watched as Tom Ireland closed the door behind him and then said aloud, 'Two clichés in one sentence, and I don't even know where *carry the can* comes from.'

Chapter Eleven

STAY ALERT

April 26th

I don't think I've seen the wife, Elise, for more than a week. Ten days, probably – several days before I tried surveillance from the cabbage patch anyway. I can't talk to Eve because she'll be angry but I am worried. I see him every now and then, usually having a cigarette, just standing there. Eve thinks I'm just nosey, but isn't that how domestic tyrants get away with it? If we all mind our own business, whose business is it to call abusers to account? Admittedly the police have changed their attitude – *just a domestic* does seem to have slipped out of their vocabulary – but there ought to be a stage before involving the police, surely? The stage where other people – family, friends, neighbours – let the abuser know that they are watching, that he can't get away with posing as a decent chap. I hesitate to hold up the sixteenth century as an ideal for marital relations because it is true that it was regarded as acceptable for a man to beat his wife if she "deserved" it, but there was a code and neighbours took action if a man overstepped the mark. The home was a much less private place and people soon knew if a man got drunk and went home to slap his wife around. And they took action. The man would be hauled out in front of everyone the next Sunday in church and given a dressing down. He'd be shamed. As I say, I'm not suggesting that being an Elizabethan wife was perfect happiness, but it is 130 years since the term *feminism* was first used in this country, and last year over 1,300,000 women were abused by their husbands or partners. Playing with numbers isn't usually my thing, but that is 10,000 women *each year* for every year we have been talking about feminism. Shouldn't someone be ashamed?

All this is a preliminary to my decision that I have to do something about Elise. I can't just stand here and look out of my window when a woman is, at the very least, under duress not fifty yards away from me. Her husband may not be violent but there is coercion going on there, of that I'm sure. I knew it the first time I saw them together with the cat. And where is the cat?

I am going to have to get closer and take a look in at the windows. He – Paul – must go out sometimes, mustn't he, for food? And his work may be mostly on hold but surely he gets called out to emergencies. It occurs to me that he must have a van, which will be parked outside the house, so I can walk round the block and check. Of course, I shall need an excuse for going out and a breath of fresh air won't do since we have only just returned from Flossie's walk. It will have to be the old standby, the letter to post, though that gets less convincing in a world of email. I use it anyway, popping my head round Freda's door to tell her.

I walk along to the corner, counting the houses, then up the road and round the next corner. I am about to count the houses along here but there is no need – I can see the van. So he's in. I walk along to take a look – there are windows at the front, after all. The van is clean and spruce, with *Paul Jessop Plumber* on it in dark blue lettering, with a mobile phone number and no jokey slogan. What there is, however, is a neat laminated notice fixed in the back window:

Due to the coronavirus
Paul Jessop Plumbing
is not trading at present

So much for my plan. And so much for any freedom for Elise.

The house is spruce like the van, a neat semi with shiny paintwork, and the garden is what I would call anally tidy. I walk up the short front drive, past the van, trying to walk quietly without looking stealthy. I shade my eyes and look in through the window. An empty sitting room, also tidy.

Under normal circumstances I would find an excuse to ring the bell – a vague plumbing enquiry or even a brazen self-introduction as a new neighbour staying with Eve Flynn – but the conventions of lockdown defeat me and I go home.

Back in my room, I consider plan B. I need an excuse for getting into the Jessops' garden. When I was down among the vegetables, I noticed a break in the fence between the two gardens, which is hardly a fence at all, really – more a sketch of a fence in the form of a row of low, wonky palings. I assume that it is Eve's and Colin's responsibility, because if it were Paul Jessop's it would be as trim as everything else in his domain. Anyway, behind the big apple tree the palings have fallen away. Maybe the tree's roots have undermined them. The idea of slipping through the gap brings me a genuine childhood memory. When I told Eve my story about going through the hedge at the end of the garden to play with friends, that was just a ploy to bring up the subject of her neighbours (and she saw through it, of course). There were no children at the end of our garden. I had very few friends at all, in fact; I was an only and a lonely child. There was one house I went to sometimes, though. The mother – Diana – was a friend of my mother's, and after my father died I used to go there if my mother was working at the weekend. Our house was an efficient little box, designed to give the least trouble to a working single mother, but Diana's house was rambling and scruffy – almost derelict in places, I think as I remember it now – and none of the fences were whole. I can conjure up now the thrill of terror as I slipped with her children into the forbidden territory of other people's gardens. And we always used the same *modus operandi* in case we were caught – we threw a ball over ahead of us. *May we have our ball back, please?* I could get away with that, couldn't I?

I do a swift recce of the house. Colin is in his study at the front of the house, out of sight of the garden; Freda and Eve are in the kitchen looking at Freda's sketches. They could see me from the window but they seem to be engrossed. I find Flossie's ball in the pile of outdoor shoes in the hall and then find Flossie, peacefully asleep in a patch of sunshine in the sitting room. She may be surprised at my sudden interest in her, but she is young and willing and puts on a good performance of eagerness as I urge her out through the French doors into the garden.

Out there, I'm the one putting on the performance, just in case I am observed, smiling cheerily, tossing the ball, praising the dog each time she retrieves it and drops it at my feet, and all the time moving further and further down the garden towards my goal. Finally we are close enough, and I chuck the ball recklessly over the fence.

What I had not reckoned with, of course, is that Flossie goes straight in after it. She knows exactly where the fence break is, and she is through it in a flash, bringing the ball back to me while I am still manoeuvring my way over the fallen palings. I take the ball from her and surreptitiously roll it back down the Jessops' garden, then walk in boldly, doing a performance of looking for a ball that is very obviously lying in the middle of the lawn.

Averting my eyes from it and scanning unlikely flowerbeds, I move up the garden. A glance through a window is all I can hope for, but it is better than nothing. I am ready with my excuse if I am caught near the house, and I need it. As soon as I am in range of a window, the back door opens and Paul Jessop comes out.

'Can I help you?' he says.

Is there the equivalent question in all languages, I wonder, used to challenge an intruder who is not obviously a burglar? Or is it a particularly British phenomenon, the passive-aggressive, polite rudeness of *Can I help you?*, delivered, as it is in these circumstances, in a calculatedly unhelpful tone?

I try to be charming. I smile in what I believe to be a winning way, and I say, 'I'm sorry for trespassing. In fact,' (*little laugh*) 'I was just going to knock at your back door to say *sorry for trespassing*! I'm Gina.'

I don't put out a hand to shake, of course, but I try to look as though I would shake hands with him in normal circumstances. He doesn't offer a name, so I offer my credentials. 'I'm staying with your neighbours for the duration – Eve and Colin.' I gesture in the direction of their house as though he might not know who I'm talking about. 'I came through the gap in the fence to retrieve this little one's ball,' I continue, gesturing now at Flossie, who has helpfully dropped the ball at my feet and is now watching us anxiously, afraid, I think, that she might be called on to do something heroic. 'I was a bit overenthusiastic about throwing it for her,' I conclude, and wait for something from him.

'Well, you've got it now,' he says. 'You could have just let the dog get it.'

'Yes, I could, couldn't I?' I give a merry little laugh. 'Anyway, I'm so sorry to have disturbed you – and your wife.'

I angle my head to look beyond him through the open back door, as though I expect to see her lurking there. Without turning round, he pushes the door closed behind him and takes a step towards me. I have been keeping more than the statutory two metres from him but I take a couple of steps back anyway. He is not a tall man but he is broad and muscly, and there is in him the quality I first noticed when I saw him smoking under the tree by the lake. He seems to be barely containing pent-up anger, and while it is annoying, I know, to find me and my dog in his garden, it is not really a reason for rage, is it? Not unless he has something to hide.

His move forward and my retreat have convinced Flossie that this is her moment to demonstrate that *though she be but little, she is fierce*. She doesn't get near him, having the sense to keep out of kicking distance, but she sets up a terrific yapping and prances about on her back legs. Time to go. I start to back off down the garden, which must look ridiculous, so I make myself turn round to walk the rest of the way, with Flossie, her ball forgotten, running ahead of me. And then I hear him call. Is he pursuing me? I am tempted to keep going, but I do turn round.

'You're the one who goes out with those girls in the mornings, aren't you?' he calls. 'My wife had to stop going running because of them. They should think about what they're doing or someone will come to harm.'

I turn and go. Was he threatening me? Threatening Freda and the girls? And then my heart somersaults as a missile comes whizzing past me. Flossie, though, scampers with delight. It is her ball.

As we get near the house, the kitchen door opens and Eve appears. She knows where I have been, of course, but she looks not so much angry as determined.

'I've made coffee,' she says, 'and we need to eat some of that cake.'

I go in, removing my muddy shoes, and sit down obediently at the kitchen table, waiting to be rebuked. When we both have coffee and cake, Eve says, 'I'll tell you what, Gina. I was a GP's wife for nearly thirty years and I learnt not to gossip – not about people's health, not about their relationships, not even about their summer holidays. I don't tell anyone's private business to anyone else. So, when you started getting interested in Paul and Elise, I thought I could just warn you off – let you know I wasn't giving you a story and hope you would lose interest. I should have known better, of course.'

'So there is a story!' I feel vindicated. 'I knew there was. He's an angry man – you can see it in him – and controlling at the very least. I saw it the first time I noticed them in the garden – unkind to the cat and coercive to her.'

She looks at me with that Irish wise woman gaze of hers and says, 'You are so wrong. So wrong.'

'What do you mean? I hope you're not going to try to tell me that she bullies him, because I simply won't—'

'There is a story,' she says, 'but it's not that one.'

'So what is it? Because as I see it, he's a nasty piece of work. Not just the way he treats her, but just now he threatened Freda and the girls?'

'He did what?'

'For weeks he hung around by the lake in the mornings and watched the girls going by, doing their singing stuff. He doesn't do it anymore, but just now, his parting shot was that the girls needed to watch out or harm would come to them.'

'Are you sure that's what he said?'

'He said his wife had had to give up running because of them and they should think about what they were doing or someone would come to harm.'

'Ah. So he didn't actually threaten them, did he?'

'As good as.'

'No. Now I'm going to tell you things you have no business knowing because it's the only way to make you stop all this, but it goes no further, right?'

'Well, if it's criminal, I—'

'It's not criminal, it's just private. Personal. Right?'

'Right.'

'Elise is prone to acute allergic reactions. A whole range of things from peanuts to cat fur can send her into anaphylactic shock. To my knowledge she's been rushed to hospital three times since they moved here.'

'OK. But I don't see —'

'Paul worries about her. She's pretty sensible about it but she can be quite stubborn. She's supposed to be shielding, of course, but she insisted on going jogging in the mornings and all Paul could do was wait nearby in case there was a crisis. She always carries an EpiPen, and he has one too. And he got her to carry a rape alarm in case she had an attack when she was out of his sight.'

'Why didn't he just run with her?'

'He's got a bad knee – he injured it in a motorbike accident when he was young, I think.'

'I don't remember seeing her out in the mornings.'

'You may not have recognised her. She wears dark glasses to protect her eyes. She's usually in a red tracksuit with the hood up.'

'We've seen her. I didn't make the link. But why did he say she had to give up jogging because of the girls?'

'Think about it. Just running past someone who ate peanut butter for breakfast is enough to bring on an attack – especially if they've got their mouth open, singing or laughing.'

'Why didn't she just go running at another time?'

'She does. She runs in the evening now it's lighter. So it wasn't fair of him to say she had to give it up. She actually liked seeing the girls – she works in a school and she misses it – but she had an episode the last time she was out in the morning; not a bad one and she used her EpiPen right away, but it scared her and she agreed to give up the morning run.'

'How do you know all this?'

'We talk most days. I've sort of mothered her a bit since she's been here. Her own mother is down south somewhere and she felt quite isolated early on. She's made friends since, but when we realised we would both be shielding, we agreed that we'd be a listening ear for one another.'

'And the cat?'

'Oh, that wretched cat. It's not theirs. Cat fur is one of her allergies. The cat belongs to the previous owners of the house. Paul had to get in a firm to deep clean the place before he and Elise could move in, but the previous owners only moved two streets away, so it keeps coming back. Elise says it doesn't affect her if she is outside with it, so she goes and talks to it when she sees it in the garden. I gather it hasn't been around recently, but I don't think for a moment that Paul has murdered it. He may well have shouted at it, though, and it's decided it's better off in its new home.'

'And you don't think that he uses her allergies as an excuse for making her do what he wants?'

'He adores her, and he's terrified of losing her. When she's at work, the staff all know what to do if she has a reaction, and he can relax, but he doesn't feel able to leave her alone at home. He could be doing some work otherwise – there are always plumbing emergencies – but he's put the whole business on hold to make sure she's safe.'

'I'll take your word for it, but he's not charming, is he?'

'You were spying on him! You hardly caught him at his best.'

'OK.' I get up. I am not embarrassed by my misinterpretation of events – I just wasn't given the right information – but I do feel deflated.

'Don't go,' Eve says. 'I've got something for you. Sit down for a moment.'

She goes out of the room and comes back with a large cotton bag stuffed full of what looks like balls of wool.

'You haven't got enough to do,' she says, plonking it down on the table, 'and I feel guilty about that. The rest of us are all busy. I've got into my stride with my pots and things because I can see tourists flooding back here as soon as lockdown is lifted, and they'll want to hold onto the summer. Freda is loving her projects – and I know it riles you that she's not involving you. And Colin is having a lovely time researching papers about COVID viruses. He must know so much by now that the BBC could hire him as their resident expert – and he'd be a lot better than some of their so-called correspondents. But you're stuck. You haven't got any teaching except for the bits of dissertations that come in, and you'd normally be preparing for your summer courses, but they're not going to happen. And I suspect that you think that if you were in London you could be contributing to the hunt for Rebecca Clarke's killer. I don't think you'd be allowed in on the case, actually, but I can see that you think you could blag your way in. And I've been feeling guilty because I persuaded you to come up here, and I'm so enjoying having you and Freda here. So,' she lays a hand on the bag, 'I have a project for you. Something practical that will really help someone – that might save lives, actually.'

I eye the bag with deep suspicion. 'What?' I ask.

'Whenever I pass a charity shop,' she says, 'I nip in to pick up balls of wool. I've got a good collection here – different colours, but all double knitting. You're going to knit a blanket – in squares. I have a friend who gets people knitting these and they are sent off to a Syrian refugee camp. I've done a couple. The brighter and more colourful, the better. Comfort and cheer. What better gift? And it's a better occupation than baking birthday cakes for dead people. Better for our waistlines, certainly.' She looks at the substantial chunk of Shakespeare's cake, which – like the magic porridge pot – seems never to grow smaller.

I protest. 'Eve, I don't knit.'

'Do you mean you don't know how to?'

'I know how to. I was taught. But I don't do it.'

'What was the last thing you knitted?'

'I knitted a shawl for Freda. It took me the whole six months that I knew Ellie was pregnant and it was a good thing I decided not to make a white one because it would have been very grey by the time it was finished, the number of times I unpicked it.'

'Well, there you are. You've had the practice. And this will be knitted in squares, so if you screw up you only have to unravel a fifteen-centimetre square. It's best done in garter stitch because then it doesn't have a right and wrong side, so you don't even have to purl. You can do simple squares, but you can get more ambitious as you get better – move on to stripes, if you want to.' She starts pulling balls of wool out of the bag. 'Look. Lovely colours. I've put needles in there for you. Forty stitches and fifty rows for each square, and an eight square by twelve blanket is best – ninety-six squares. If you can manage one a day, that will take you to the end of July, when we expect to be released!'

I am speechless, incapable of resistance. I can't help feeling that this is my penance for busybodying over the neighbours, but thus it was that Eve used to get recalcitrant teenagers to do penance for misdemeanours by tidying the cupboards and scrubbing the sinks in her art room. And how can I refuse to send comfort and cheer? I am already picturing my blanket, glowing with goodwill in the misery of a makeshift camp. I talk too much and do too little. I shall do my penance.

'Thank you,' I say meekly. 'I shall go and sit with Flossie in the other room, and be one of *the spinsters and the knitters in the sun.*'

'Where's that from?'

'*Twelfth Night*. When Orsino is requesting a particular

87

song from Feste. He says *The spinsters and the knitters in the sun, and the free maids that weave their thread with bones do use to chant it*. It's interesting really, because he is surrounded by men in his court, but what he's asking for is a women's song.'

'And what is the song?'

'It's a gloomy dirge of a song, actually – *Come away death*. Orsino is being all self-indulgent about his broken heart.'

'Well, if you're intending to sing while you work, I hope you'll sing something cheerful.'

'I shan't sing. But I will need something to entertain me once I get into the swing of it.'

'Radio Four.' Eve hands me the little solar-powered radio that stands on the kitchen windowsill. 'Here you are. You'll be an expert on everything by the time you've finished.'

I pick up the bag and the radio. 'How many stitches did you say?'

'Forty. Do you remember how to cast on?'

'I shall work it out,' I say haughtily.

In the sitting room, sharing Flossie's patch of sunshine by the French doors, I set the radio down but don't switch it on; I need to concentrate fully on the casting on. After a couple of fumbles, the thumb method comes back to me and I get started. I am still not ready for Radio Four, though.

I have a problem with Radio Four these days. I still love it; I have loved it since I was thirteen and was in hospital having my tonsils out. I had been put in a women's ward and my fellow patients were old and terrifying, wired and tubed in various alarming ways. Even I couldn't read all the time, so resorting to the radio headphones above my bed was a comfort and I was hooked. Radio Four has been my companion ever since. I can do the litany of my favourites: *The Today Programme, The World at One* and *PM; In Our Time* and *The Long View; The Life Scientific* and *More or Less; Open Book, Book Club* and *Book at Bedtime; Desert Island Discs* and

Woman's Hour; The News Quiz, Dead Ringers, The Now Show and *I'm Sorry I Haven't a Clue*. It has its weaknesses and you will notice the omissions in my list: *Any Questions* and *Any Answers* depress me. *Down the Line* is a brilliant phone-in parody but the line between parody and reality is perilously fine. Most of the daytime drama is pretty terrible and some of the six-thirty comedy is execrable. And I used to be devoted to *The Archers* but I fell out of love with it when it came under new management. So there we are. Those are my prejudices. Please don't phone in with your comments.

Actually, for me the real problem with Radio Four is that it deceives. It deceives me into believing that the people for whom these programmes are created are the real Britain – that what we are at heart are the thoughtful, earnest, open-minded people the Beeb believes us to be – well-informed, well-read, well-intentioned. And this is not true. 21% of us listen to Radio Four, and even among those who do, there will be some who have voted to turn Britain into an irrelevant, fractured off-shore island, pursuing a fantasy of greatness and sinking into economic stasis. (Once again, please don't phone in.)

I would switch the radio on at this point, but I see that it is twelve-thirty, and I really can't be doing with *You and Yours*.

Chapter Twelve

SELF-ISOLATION

April 28th

Freda was thinking about marriage. Amy and Robert Dudley's marriage in particular. Colin had given her a sort of answer to the first of the four questions she had set herself: the fact that the Dudleys didn't have any children didn't necessarily mean that they didn't have a proper marriage. So the next question was why, if everyone knew that they were married, were there so many rumours that the queen was going to marry Robert? The *Elizabeth* film had partly got round that problem by pretending that the queen didn't know that he was married, but that obviously wasn't true. Freda's theory was that if you were the queen, you could behave as though the world was as you wanted it to be and it would magically become like that. Hadn't Henry VIII been the same? First it was all right for him to be married to Catherine of Aragon and then it wasn't, then Anne Boleyn was a witch and a tart and Anne of Cleeves, who looked perfectly all right in the pictures of her, was too hideous to be married to. So Freda thought that the queen simply behaved as though Robert was free to marry, and everyone else went along with it because she was the queen.

People did try to work out how the queen was actually going to get what she wanted. There were obviously lots of rumours going round – that Amy was very ill and likely to die, and that Robert was planning to poison her. Freda didn't believe the illness story, partly because the coroner would have noticed the 'malady of the breast', wouldn't he? And also there were the clothes. It was clear from the book she was reading that although Amy wasn't allowed to be at court, she lived quite a luxurious life away from her husband. The Wikipedia entry about her said that she lived with friends in various parts of the country, and it made her sound as though she was a sort of poor relation, being taken in by friends – almost like she was sofa surfing. But it wasn't like that at all. She had her own staff of servants – a *retinue* – about ten of them, who travelled around with her, and at Cumnor Place, where she died, she had her own separate apartment, and her host was a sort of hanger-on of the Dudleys, so he had to make sure she was comfortable. And the clothes. In her book, Christine Hartweg had examples of the bills that Robert paid for velvet dresses and silks and gold adornments. Amy wouldn't have wanted those if she never went anywhere, would she? She must have been having a social life. And if she was dressing up and having a social life then she wasn't desperately ill, was she? And paying all those bills made Freda think that Robert must still have loved his wife. Or did he just feel guilty?

Amy and Robert did have a home of their own, in Hertfordshire. Freda was a bit hazy about where Hertfordshire was but she thought it wasn't far from London, and it seemed that Robert had visited Amy there. So why did she go travelling round, staying in other people's houses? Freda could only guess, but she thought it was probably just too lonely to be living alone with just her servants, and probably at that time she wouldn't have been able to go out to parties and things on her own. It was better to be staying with friends so she could do things with them.

So one question was, why was Amy so determined to be on her own on the day she died? You could understand her giving her servants time off to go to the fair. That was probably what kind masters and mistresses did. Freda could remember an episode of *Downton Abbey* where all the servants went to the fair. But Amy tried to persuade the other people who lived in the house to go too. They didn't go, so the whole house wasn't empty, like some of the accounts suggested – just Amy's part. So, people assumed that if Amy was trying to get rid of everyone so she could be on her own, it was because she was planning to kill herself, but actually if her plan was to throw herself down the stairs, she didn't need the house to be empty really. It wasn't as though her servants would have followed her round all the time. So all she would have needed was to wait for a quiet moment and then go out and do it. If Amy really did deliberately clear her part of the house, then it was much more likely that she wanted to do something secret, and the most likely thing Freda could think of was that she was expecting a secret visit from someone.

One thing that made Freda think that Amy was wanting to look her best at that time – early September 1560 – was that she wrote a letter to her tailor in London, ordering a new collar to be put on a dress that he had just made for her. Her letter made quite a fuss about the sort of collar – the same as he had put on another dress for her – and she stressed that she wanted it sent with as much speed as he could. It looked to Freda as though Amy was very keen to look her best for some occasion that was coming up, wanting to wear her new gown and wanting a collar on it that she thought suited her. Could she have been expecting a visit from Robert?

If Robert ever visited Amy, he would have had to do it secretly so the queen didn't find out, wouldn't he? Robert was Master of the Queen's Horse, so he would have had no trouble getting good horses. Could he have ridden up to

Cumnor to see her? Freda didn't think it was at all likely that he killed her, because you could tell from the letter that he wrote after she died that he got into quite a panic, thinking that everyone would suspect him of murdering her. But suppose he promised to come and Amy got all prepared, sending the servants off and putting her new dress on, and then he didn't come. Would that have been enough to make her jump from the stairs in despair? Or he could have come but they might have had a row, and she could have despaired after he had gone. There was one more scenario that was suggesting itself to Freda's mind, too, but she was going to have to think more about that.

While she was still pondering, Granny came in. She had a way of saying *Knock, knock* and opening the door at the same time, so there was never any chance to say, *Just a minute* or *Don't come in*. Still, as Freda had to remind herself, this was a lot more privacy than she would have had sharing a room with Nico.

Granny actually looked slightly embarrassed.

'You wouldn't have such a thing as some crayons, would you?' she asked.

'Crayons? Are you doing a home-made birthday card for someone, Granny?' she asked.

'It's for my knitting. I think I need to draw out a design. I decided that just knitting random squares isn't going to work.'

Freda opened the drawer of the dressing table that she was using as a desk. 'I don't have crayons, but I have felt pens or Sharpies.'

'What are Sharpies?'

'Like marker pens.'

'I'll go for felt pens. I'm used to them. You don't have any squared paper, I suppose?'

'Will graph paper do?'

'It might. This really isn't my kind of thing, you know. I'm in *terra incognita* here.'

'It's very good for you. Learning new things when you're getting old keeps your brain active.'

'Well, thank you, Freda. I'll bear that in mind as I hobble back downstairs to my knitting.'

'I'm happy to give you a hand if you need it.'

'No. My finished blanket will be a surprise – like your project.'

'OK,' Freda said. 'Whatever.'

Chapter Thirteen

COVIDEO

May 1ˢᵗ

Freda has sent me an email, forwarding a Facebook post. I look at the subject line for a long time before I steel myself to open it. *OUR REBECCA* is the line, and I know what this is. Rebecca Clarke's family, thwarted by COVID rules of a proper farewell to their beloved girl, have refused to bury her *hugger-mugger* and have turned the photos, the memories and the eulogies into a video. They may have intended it only for family and friends but that's not the way it works. It is out in the world, and now it is sitting in my inbox. I don't want to open it. I don't want to feel like a voyeur and I don't want to weep, but my message to myself is the same as it always is, confronted with bombings, drownings, fires and other devastation: *If they have to endure it, the least you can do is witness it.* So here it is.

It is very professional in the way it has been put together, and I remember that Rebecca's father works in IT. It starts with video clips, seamlessly woven together, from babyhood to adolescence, paddling pools to diving from the high board, uncertain first steps to a ballet solo. Watching Rebecca playing with her younger sister, little blonde muppets, I can't help being reminded of my own two girls, though I never took videos of them; I was content enough if they weren't damaging themselves or one another. I didn't need a record of their survival. After the clips come the tributes. Her parents don't appear, but her sister is there, bravely, with the tears streaming down her face, saying, *'Becks was always there for me. She led the way and she made every new step seem easy – starting school, making friends, going to secondary, doing exams – it was like she was always there, holding my hand, telling me it would be all right. And now I have to go through the world on my own.'* She is followed by Rebecca's friends, filmed standing in a COVID-distanced circle outside initially, and then appearing one by one to say the same things over and over – that Rebecca was brilliant but she never made other people feel bad, that she would do anything for her friends, and – with a particular emphasis I feel but don't understand – that she never forgot old friends and was always kind, even to people who others laughed at. After this came her teachers – the coach of the athletics team, followed by the deputy head. Deputy heads are absurdly young these days, I note. He speaks of Rebecca as a *golden girl* who embraced the promise of the world ahead of her, and he reads, very well, *Fear no more the heat of the sun* from Shakespeare's *Cymbeline: Golden lads and girls all must / As chimney sweepers come to dust.*

I manage not to weep at this by distracting myself with thoughts of chimney sweepers. For years I thought that the reference here was chimney sweeps, so blackened that they seemed to be made of coal dust. I suppose I was thinking anachronistically of Dickensian children, going up the high Victorian chimneys, though there was no need for them to sweep the chimneys in the low-ceilinged houses of Shakespeare's time. And then I learnt that dandelion seed heads (which I remember calling *dandelion clocks*) were called *chimney sweepers*, and that made so much more sense – the golden dandelions collapsing into the dusty seed heads, floating away on the wind. I wonder if Philip Murano, the deputy head who reads the poem so well, has this picture in his mind. He is close to breaking down as he finishes, I can see, and a pretty woman – his wife, I suppose – appears behind him, putting a hand on his shoulder and looking out, briefly, at the camera before we move on. We move on to a stony-faced middle-aged couple, who turn out to be the headmaster and his wife, sitting together on a sofa in a very beige sitting room. Why she is there, I don't know. She is larger than him – not taller, maybe, but definitely broader, with a large head and broad features, while he is scrawny, thin-faced and thin-lipped, and I realise that the expression on his face is one of terror. Perhaps the wife is there to stop him from running away. He looks into the camera as though it is the barrel of a gun and creaks out a few platitudes – *a conscientious student... popular with her peers... a valued member of the school community... will be missed*. The remarks are so generic, so non-specific, that I wonder if he knew Rebecca at all. When he finishes, his wife leans forward to turn the camera off, and the look on her face is startlingly unguarded for a moment. I think she is so disappointed in this man that she actually hates him.

He is the last speaker, but fortunately the video doesn't end with him. Enter selected members of the school choir in which Rebecca sang. They have recorded themselves, I suppose, as Freda and the other girls did for their video, and someone has put them together. Looking achingly young and solemn, they sing *You'll Never Walk Alone* followed by *Abide With Me*, and I drip tears all over my computer keyboard.

Without really thinking about it, I phone both my girls. Ellie mainly wants news of Freda.

'She's quite sparing with her news,' she says. 'Is she all right?'

I say, 'She's very happy, I think,' and then add, hastily, 'She's missing you, of course, but she's got plenty to do, and she's still seeing the other girls. But she's just getting to that secretive stage, you know, where she wants some things to be private. She won't say a word to me about her History project, for instance.'

'The one about Amy Robsart, you mean?'

Amy Robsart! So that's it. And why keep that secret from me? There are all sorts of things I could tell her about that story.

'Yes, Amy Robsart,' I say. 'Good choice. She doesn't tell me much. I assume she's doing all her research online.'

'I guess.'

'I just hope she knows how to sort the good info from the dodgy.'

'That's the object of the exercise, isn't it? She's right not to ask you anything because she can't check your sources.'

Thank you, Ellie. 'How are things there?' I ask. 'Is Nonna still in sole charge of the kitchen?'

'*Certamente.* Ben says I should embrace it; I should think for how many years I shall be making three meals a day for four people and regard this as a sabbatical. So I'm trying. And I have managed to do a bit of baking with Nico. Maddalena and Enrico have got addicted to some of the late-afternoon quizzes on TV, so we slip into the kitchen then, before Maddalena is ready to start on supper.'

'How's Nico doing?'

'Not bad. He's a bit bored and missing having other kids to play with, but little boys don't have those intense friendships that girls have, I think. And Ben and Enrico have got him involved with the vegetable plot, and he's quite excited about seeing things grow. I'm only just realising properly how bright he is. Most of the work that's set from school is too easy for him really.'

'Is he brighter than Freda?'

'Different. He's a whizz at maths. Ben was always good at maths, apparently.'

I feel oddly calmed and reassured by the ordinariness of this conversation, and by managing not to put a foot wrong with Ellie. I quit while I'm ahead.

'I was planning to ring and see how Annie is,' I say. 'Have you heard from her recently?'

'Yes. Domestic bliss is beginning to pall a bit, I think. But don't say *I told you so.*'

'Would I?' I say.

Actually, Annie sounds much brighter than I expect, and when I ask how things are going, she says, 'Getting better all the time. Jon sometimes gets to sleep a whole night at home.'

'The numbers are dropping, aren't they?'

'They are, and they're finding better treatments, so he is happier.'

'And he appreciates being looked after?'

'He does. And I have some news, actually.'

'You're not pregnant, are you?' The words are out before I can bite down and suppress them. *Stupid, stupid, stupid. If she is pregnant, what is the point of my letting her know that I think it's a bad idea? And isn't it up to her anyway?*

Amazingly, she laughs. 'No! I've had conversations about this with my friends. We all agree that for mothers with daughters approaching thirty, that is the only news they want to hear – or don't want to, in your case, it seems.'

'I didn't mean—' I start to backtrack, but she cuts me off.

'We're not ready for that yet, but my news is a sort of preliminary.'

'You're getting married?'

'Oh, Ma. For a woman who thinks of herself as a radical, you can be amazingly conventional.'

'So what, then?'

'I'm going to do the Scottish bar exams. It's quite a performance because Scottish law is different, but we've decided that we're here to stay. This feels like a much better place than England at the moment. Independence will come – it has to. Brexit has finished the union. And we want to be in the EU. We can all see that the Westminster government's making a complete bollocks of a trade agreement. England's finished.'

'I can't disagree with you. Can I come too?'

'Of course! Plenty of work for an English teacher in EU Scotland.'

'No. It's a tempting idea but I'm too old for a fresh start. I'll just wallow around here, clinging to the wreckage. I do envy you the sainted Nicola, though, compared with what we've got in the way of leadership here.'

'I can't tell you how much people despise him here.'

'You don't need to.'

'And how are you, Ma?' she asks. 'Are you coping with it all?'

I am struck dumb. Nearly thirty years it has been, and I don't believe that Annie has ever before asked me how I am. My role has been to listen to the woes and frustrations that comprise the drama of Annie's life, to sympathise, to advise at my peril and, quite often, to take the blame. I didn't believe that she had ever thought of me as someone who might have woes of my own.

I swallow. 'I'm fine,' I say. 'Hunky dory. But thank you for asking.'

'I worry about you,' she says, 'because you need an audience, don't you?'

Since I'm in catch-up mode, when I put the phone down from talking to Annie, I call Lavender. She has been preying on my mind from time to time. I half thought that she would take up my offer and ring me for a heart-to-heart but I have heard nothing and I fear that she may be so overwhelmed that she has lost the will to save herself. So I am extremely surprised when she answers the phone sounding very bright and bouncy. *Medication?* I wonder. But no.

'Gina!' she says. 'Lovely to hear from you. I've been worried about you stuck there with the virus simply raging. Are you all right?'

'Stuck where, Lavender?'

'Well, aren't you in London?'

'No, actually.'

'Are you in Scotland with Annie?'

'You know about that?'

'She rang Andrew. Something about Scottish law.'

'Well, I'm in Carnmere.'

'Remind me where that is?'

'The Lake District.'

'Oh, lovely!'

I feel a need to soften the fact that I chose Eve's invitation over hers. 'I'm helping a friend out,' I say. 'She's shielding. And I have Freda with me – she has friends up here. They do synchronised dog walking.'

'Lovely!' she cries again. 'Actually, I do synchronised riding with a couple of friends, which is super.'

'So you're not on twenty-four-hour child-minding duties?'

'Oh, I have to tell you, Gina, I think I have been really quite clever.'

Her tone suggests that she is as surprised as I am at the possibility of her being clever.

She goes on. 'I took your advice and asked Mummy and Daddy to come and stay. They said no at first, but then Mrs Deakin, who has cleaned Mummy's house *forever*, announced that she wouldn't be coming in during the lockdown – wanted to be *furloughed*, if you please! And Mummy realised that she couldn't possibly manage that house all on her own, so they're here, ensconced in our guest room, with their en suite and everything, and it's all lovely.'

'Except that you're cleaning and cooking for six people, presumably?'

'Well, that's not so bad, you know. Mummy is very good about looking after their room and bathroom, and you know, I've had a lifetime of mucking out stables, so cleaning a house is a doddle by comparison!'

'It would be,' I say. 'And do your parents help with the boys?'

'Well, not that much. They find them rather tiring, actually, but Gina,' she drops her voice to a conspiratorial whisper, 'Andrew is a transformed man.'

'Really!'

'And I'm so glad I took your advice about inviting Mummy and Daddy.'

Did I advise her to invite them? I think I may have wished her luck with that, but it's not the same thing, is it?

'Because,' she goes on, 'you were quite right when you said to me once that Andrew liked to have everything his own way, but he also wanted to be admired. So with Mummy and Daddy here, he wants to be the perfect son-in-law. And he can do it, Gina. I thought he couldn't help being like he is, you know – inconsiderate, really, and quite cross a lot of the time – but he has kept it up for weeks – being nice to me and playing with the boys and helping them with school work. Mummy and Daddy think he's wonderful.'

'He must be ready to explode,' I say. 'The moment lockdown is lifted he'll invent an urgent case in South America and disappear to recuperate.'

'Oh probably, but he'll have served his purpose by then, won't he?'

Is it very unusual for two women to have this kind of conversation about a shared once and current husband? I do feel that it is a tribute to both of us. I am also delighted to think how furious Andrew would be if he knew.

'I salute you, Lavender,' I say. 'You've got the measure of him.'

'Thank you,' she says. 'You know, men are more like horses than I realised.'

It is not often that Lavender says anything that gives me food for thought but when I come off the phone I find myself thinking about that last remark and, more generally, about how couples manage one another. It is mid-morning but no-one else is in the kitchen when I go to put the kettle on, so I avert my eyes from the cake tin, make a cup of instant coffee and take it back upstairs with me. Then, sitting in the rather comfortable basket chair that Eve has put in my room, I run over my morning's exposure to couple dynamics.

First the teachers – the headmaster and the deputy head, and their wives. It is ridiculous to leap to judgement, I know, on the basis of a few seconds of video, but I am pretty sure that the headmaster is a man of straw, and his substantial wife keeps him propped up. But she is tired of it; this may not be what she bargained for and she is a disappointed woman. The deputy's wife isn't disappointed; she is as good-looking and polished as he is. They are on the up. There was something challenging in her look, though, but perhaps that's the natural reflex for the wife of a very good-looking man.

Moving on to couples I actually know, I think about Ellie and Ben. Ellie was only twelve when Andrew and I divorced, but perhaps she had seen enough to know what sort of man not to marry. She was not in a strong position when she met Ben – the single mother of a small daughter of uncertain paternity. Plenty of men would have exploited that to make her feel grateful for being rescued, but Ben admires Ellie as well as loving her. He copes with her occasional histrionics; she copes with his obsessiveness about his music.

Annie, of course, demands admiration, as well as going for gold in histrionics. I have always been afraid that Jon would just get exhausted by her. I have known him since he was nobbut a lad, but he was mature and sensible even then. I can only suppose that he finds his own good sense unexciting and welcomes the emotional ups and downs that life with Annie offers. You might think that being a cardiologist would offer challenges enough, but clearly not. And possibly, just possibly, Annie is seeing that there are greater challenges than the dramas of her daily life.

And Lavender. Egotist that I am, I have always thought that Andrew married Lavender because she is everything I am not. I was his template for the wrong sort of wife, and Lavender fitted the obverse template – young, while I was approaching middle age; rich, rather than earning a state school teacher's pittance; well-connected, while I despised Andrew's desire to hobnob with the county gentry; educationally challenged, while I was egregiously well-educated; compliant, where I was stroppy; sweet, while I was sour. Well, this is all true, but it turns out that Lavender, though not clever by my standards, has cunning, and though not stroppy, has a powerful instinct for survival. All credit to the horses, I would say.

So this – my failure to manage Andrew – leads me inexorably to the long-running question of my relationship with David; to the question, in fact, of why we can't manage really to be a couple at all. I notice in passing that my catch-up session with people I love/feel responsible for has not included David. That is because he would assume that I was ringing for information on the hunt for a murderer, and he would mainly be right, but it doesn't stop me from thinking about him. I have a friend (divorced twice) who says that successful marriages/partnerships are showbusiness – one is the show and the other is the business. It's a model that doesn't always work, but think about couples that you know and you will find it is very often true. Whether people know that is the role they are taking on from the start, I can't say. Sometimes, I guess, they fill the vacant space. And if they can't? Well, if both halves of the couple are business, I suppose that can work – it would just be a bit dull. If both want to be the show – well, that's where Andrew and I foundered. He grabbed the limelight with his cases at The Hague and I resented the business – everything from 24/7 child management to calling in plumbers to being a *plus one* at almost all social occasions. Looking back, I can't say exactly what sort of star I expected to be – I just felt entitled to a bit of shining. I had done some acting at university, and I would have liked to do some amateur theatre, but Andrew was away so much and I couldn't afford the babysitters. But that wasn't really the problem; I just wanted a bit of admiration from Andrew, I think. I wanted to be a star at home.

I suppose my amateur meddling in matters of murder has been a bid to be the show in recent years, and possibly my problems with David are as simple as that. David is not a show-off in the way that I am; he is quite low-key and self-effacing, uncomfortable in the public eye delivering media statements and so on, but what I think I have not really registered is that, in the police force, David is a star. On the odd occasions when I am invited to don evening dress and go as his guest into the glamorous world of the Metropolitan Police top brass, I am reliably regaled by overweight middle-aged men with descriptions of David as a *young Turk*, and tributes to his astuteness, professionalism and flair. *Flair?* That is supposed to be what I have, in my amateur way, while David does the routine police procedural stuff; but in the world of the Met, David has flair all of his own. So that's the problem. We can put on a pretty good performance as a duo, but we are always elbowing each other for the star billing. Well, too bad. It works, doesn't it? And if it's not a pattern for domestic bliss, so be it, I suppose.

After all this, I nearly pick up my phone to call him, but if he hasn't actually got anywhere with the case and I have nothing to admire, where will that get us? I drain my coffee, wishing that I'd bothered with the real stuff, and turn on my laptop. While it is waking up, I complete my relationship roundup with thoughts closer to home. Colin and Eve? Easy. Eve is, of course, the show, and Colin has always seemed quite happy with that. And Paul and Elise? It seemed that he was the show, all power and control while she hovered like a wraith, mainly out of sight, but Eve's account changes that; maybe she and her allergies and the way she does or doesn't deal with them lie at the heart of that marriage and he is the business – keeping her alive.

As I watch my emails popping in I have one more thought. Amy Robsart and Robert Dudley. Now there was a showbusiness marriage if ever there was one: he the royal favourite, the preening cock of the walk at Elizabeth's court, and she the dirty little secret, the rashly married, inconvenient wife, hidden away from the public eye. Does Freda see this? Isn't she too young to understand a marriage? Wouldn't she like my help?

Chapter Fourteen

INCUBATION

May 3rd

'How do you feel about Josh Clements as our suspect, Tom?' David Scott asked. 'Gut instinct?'

Tom Ireland had called in for his habitual end-of-the-day debrief on the Rebecca Clarke case and they were sitting in easy chairs by the window of Scott's third-floor office as the building emptied below them. From ground level they could hear the muffled sounds of car doors slamming and *goodnights* being called. It was still light, though, with the teasing, chilly brightness of early spring evenings.

Tom Ireland slapped the file that lay on his lap. 'Gut instinct, he's not our boy,' he said.

'But he's all we've got?'

'He is. And we've got possible motive – obsession with Rebecca, who was out of his league, threatening text messages from his phone, only alibi his mother, and electric flex with Rebecca's DNA on it in the recycling bin in his front garden.'

'So put yourself in the Defence's shoes and tell me why those don't add up.'

'First, motive. Rebecca's friends insist that she was always nice to him. She wasn't going to go out with him, but she never "cancelled" him, like the text messages say. So then that casts doubt on the texts. And from the statement from the headmaster's secretary, we can see that it wouldn't have been difficult for another pupil to have picked up his phone.'

'Explain.'

'Confiscated phones are kept in the safe in the head's secretary's office, where they keep exam papers and such. They're put in labelled envelopes. At the end of the school day they go and pick them up. There's a sign-in sheet, and they sign when they claim their phone. Usual practice is that the secretary watches them as they do it, but she admits that on that day, when they were about to close for the lockdown, she was very busy and she left them to take their phones and sign without her monitoring it.'

Scott felt a small pulse of excitement. 'So, if someone else took it they would be likely to be on that sign-in sheet. They went to collect their own phone, spotted the envelope with Josh's name on it and grabbed the chance to make trouble with it.'

'Maybe. But it might not have been chance. Someone could have been there when the phone was confiscated and made a plan.'

'Except how could anyone know that Josh wouldn't collect the phone himself? Why didn't he collect it, by the way?'

'He's a dozy beggar. He forgot. It's happened before, apparently. His mother says his concentration is poor and when he gets bored in class he gets the phone out. Then when it's taken, he forgets to pick it up. It annoys her because she never knows whether she'll be able to contact him or not.'

'We need to find out the circumstances of the phone being confiscated. Who was there? And has the secretary still got the sign-in sheet?'

Tom Ireland patted his file. 'We've got it,' he said. 'Six boys' names on there, besides Josh's. Lucy Murano – that's the head's secretary – was interesting about those boys. She says it's the same ones time after time. She knows the kids quite well – she's married to the deputy head and their own kids are at the school. She says they all know they're likely to get their phones confiscated but they're addicted to them. The girls are the ones who are insecure and need to keep texting their friends to make sure that they still are friends, and the boys are mainly ADHD, like Josh, and start playing games as soon as they get bored.'

'She didn't make any suggestion about who she thought might have taken the phone?'

'No. But we've got a handwriting expert on it, looking for similarities with Josh's name on the list, and comparing his name there with examples from his school exercise books. It's quite a childish hand, his; quite easy to copy, I'd say.'

'You say six boys' names. You don't think a girl could have done it?'

'Strangling? And what would be the motive?'

'Jealousy? It would explain the absence of sexual assault, wouldn't it? And the flex was thrown round her neck from behind. It might not have needed that much strength to overpower her.'

'And get her into the river?'

'There are some quite powerful seventeen-year-old girls. Take a look at the athletics team.'

'It's not likely.'

'Don't discount it.'

There was a silence. Scott said, 'So go on with the defence case. What about his alibi?'

'His mother would be a gift to a defence counsel. Sensible woman. Loves her son but knows his limitations. And Rebecca's mother is one of her best friends. She loved the girl – knew her since she was a toddler. If she thought her son had killed her, I reckon she would turn him in.'

'She'd be a member of a very small club, then. Wives, girlfriends, mothers, sisters, they stand by their men, don't they? Everything from wilful blindness to deliberate complicity.'

Tom Ireland shrugged. 'Maybe,' he said. 'Maybe she dumped the electric flex in the bin, though it was a pretty stupid thing to do.'

'Did your team check how many litter bins there are between that stretch of river and their home?'

Ireland opened his file and flicked through. 'Five,' he said. 'We searched them all. There's a dog shit bin just near where we think it happened, then he'd have gone through the car park, and there are two bins there. And he had to walk the length of the high street and there are two bins there. Plus the other bins in gardens in their road.'

'So if Josh dropped it into the bin at home, we would have to assume that he was so traumatised by what he had done that he walked home with it in his hand and only realised that he had still got it when he reached home, and then panicked and dumped it.'

'Which doesn't fit with the murder being premeditated – as it was. Who carries electric flex around with them?'

'So you think leaving the flex there was part of the plan to incriminate Josh? You've drawn a blank on people wanting to hurt Rebecca. Should you be looking at people who might want to hurt Josh?'

'I think it's all part of the same thing. There's a boy who felt spurned by Rebecca. In these weird conditions, his feelings fester and get out of control. Maybe he starts stalking her on her early morning runs. There was something her mother said in passing when she first went missing. She said she couldn't stop thinking about the fact that Rebecca had said she thought she might stop the early morning runs, and if only she had, she would still be here. Why was she going to give up? She didn't tell anyone she was being stalked, but perhaps she was.'

'And Marcia Clements says her son doesn't get up in the mornings.'

'Exactly. And Rebecca was always nice to Josh. Maybe she cold-shouldered someone else and they resented Josh enough to frame him. And on that point, there's an odd thing. You know we have Rebecca's phone intact because it was in a waterproof case? Well, plenty of Rebecca's own DNA and fingerprints were found on her clothes, and on her phone, but none at all on the phone case.'

'Suggesting that the phone was put into the case by someone else to ensure that we got to see the text messages. That's a cool-headed killer. Any DNA or fingerprints on the case at all?'

'No. But we're pretty sure he was wearing gloves.'

'Have you asked Rebecca's parents if they recognise the case?'

'They say they don't, and they never saw the phone in a case, but she could have got it when she was doing her DofE award.'

'But why put the phone in a case to go jogging? She wasn't planning to go in the water, was she? And it wasn't a wet day. She didn't expect to get drenched. It makes no sense.' He stood up. 'Right, Tom. You've convinced me. Josh Clements isn't our boy. We're looking for a cool customer with an obsession. Move as fast as you can on that list of boys who picked up phones. And do me a favour – include the girls too. And take another look at Rebecca's ex-boyfriend. I know everyone says the split was amicable, but you never know. What's his alibi?'

'The same as Clements – still in bed at that hour of the morning, like 98% of the school population at the moment. And I can't see how he could have got hold of Josh's phone.'

'Someone could have got it for him. This was a planned thing, wasn't it? There's nothing *heat of the moment* about it. He – or she – has made some mistakes, though, and we'll get them.'

111

Chapter Fifteen

VULNERABLE PATIENT

May 4ᵗʰ

Freda was contemplating suicide. Standing on the tenth step of the staircase, she looked down and wondered whether it would be likely to kill her if she stepped off into space. *Would you step off, actually? Or throw yourself in a kind of dive?* Now she was up here she couldn't imagine how someone could actually do it.

When she had found, in the coroner's report, that the staircase that killed Amy Dudley consisted of only eight steps, she had thought that didn't seem high enough to be lethal. If you were a professional killer, wouldn't you choose a more sure-fire method than that? And if she had thrown herself down, might that have been meant more as a cry for help, but she was unlucky and hit her head? The report did say that the staircase was steep, so she was standing on the tenth step here, to be realistic and it was quite a long way down and you would hurt yourself quite a bit. She wasn't going to try it – she wasn't that stupid – but would it kill you?

'Freda, what are you doing?' Colin's voice interrupted her thoughts, sharp and anxious. He had come out of his study and was standing watching her, his face creased with worry.

'I was just thinking,' she said, 'about someone throwing themselves down stairs.'

'Let's have a chat,' he said. 'Why don't we go in here?'

He ushered her into his study and found her a chair. For a moment she thought that he was going to sit at his desk and it would be like being in the doctor's surgery, but he pulled his chair round to sit beside her. He looked rather pale, she noticed.

'Can you tell me what's the matter, Freda?'

'Nothing's the matter. It's just – it's so difficult, you know, to work out what really happened to her. Whether it was just an accident, or she meant to—'

He interrupted. 'Who is *she*?'

'Amy Dudley. You remember – I asked you about her having no children?'

'Yes, yes.' The colour was coming back into his face.

She looked at him. 'You didn't think that I was going to...? Oh, I'm sorry. I must have given you a shock.'

'You did rather.'

'But I don't have any reason to be suicidal, do I? I'm having a lovely time here.'

'I'm very glad. But in my experience, you can never be sure – especially with teenage girls.'

'Oh, our hormones, you mean. No. It's Amy who had good reason to be suicidal. She may have been ill and her husband wanted to be free to marry the queen. She died from falling down a flight of stairs in the dark. The coroner said it was an accident but she might have been trying to kill herself or she might have been pushed. I suppose the floor at the bottom was stone, so it would have been a hard fall – harder than falling onto carpet. Anyway, her neck was broken and she had two head injuries. The coroner could only measure them by his thumb – so one was a quarter of a thumb deep, and the other two thumbs, which sounds—'

She stopped. He had made an odd noise and had his hand over his eyes. He got up, nearly knocking his chair over. 'Tea time, I think,' he said. 'I'll put the kettle on.'

113

She stood up too and watched him almost stumble out of the room. Was he ill? He couldn't have been upset by her talking about head wounds, could he? He was a doctor after all. Unsure what to do, she hovered in the hall, catching glimpses of him in the kitchen, anxious that he might be going to have a stroke or something. She should tell Eve that something was wrong, she thought, and when he came to the kitchen door and said, 'Tea up', in a not-quite-normal voice, she said, 'Shall I take Eve's out to her?' and carried her own and Eve's mugs out to her shed.

'Do you mind if I come in?' she asked when Eve opened the door.

'Of course not, darling. Is it your sketches you want to talk about?'

'It's Colin,' she said. 'I'm afraid I've upset him. Or perhaps he's not well. I don't …'

Eve took her mug from her hand, which had started shaking, and sat her down on a wooden chest. 'Tell me,' she said.

Freda took a deep breath, taking in the smells that were Eve's workshop – raw wood and earthy clay and the sharp hit of paint and white spirit and the warm familiarity of fresh paper, mingled with the steamy aroma of their herbal tea. Feeling steadier, she said, 'I was talking to him about Amy Dudley – Amy Robsart, you know. You ordered the book for me.'

'And what happened?'

'He sort of broke down – went very pale and sort of stumbled out.'

Eve stood up. 'I'd better go and see him. He must be ill,' she said.

'I don't think so. He went and made the tea, and then he looked a bit better.'

Eve sat back on her stool. 'So you think it was something you said? What did you say, exactly?'

114

'I was telling him about how Amy died – falling down stairs or being pushed – and about the coroner's report and her head injuries. Because he's a doctor and I thought –'

She stopped. Now it was Eve's turn to have her hands over her face. 'Amy Robsart,' she whispered. 'I'd forgotten. Stupid. Stupid.'

She stood up, went and looked out of the window and then came back to Freda.

'I'm going to tell you something,' she said. 'Let's take a walk down the garden. It's easier to walk and talk,' she said when they got outside. 'I'm going to tell you something that I should have told you before. Last summer. You remember you wanted to know what had happened in Marlbury with Colin and the police?'

Freda felt a spurt of anger. *That again.* 'Of course I remember,' she said, 'and everyone seemed to know about it except me.'

'I know, and I'm sorry, but it's Colin's story really, not mine. But I'm going to tell you now – some of it, anyway.'

'Because I can't be trusted with the whole story?'

'Because it's complicated and it took me a long time to forgive Colin, and I don't want you to think badly of him.'

'I might imagine something worse than the truth.'

'Let me tell you, and we'll see. I think you know that there was a girl who died in Marlbury – ten years ago now. Well, Colin found her dead. She was lying at the bottom of a flight of stairs, with head injuries, so you see why –'

'But why is it a secret?'

'Colin rang the police, of course, but when they came he didn't tell them the whole truth about what had happened.'

'What had happened?'

'She had been murdered – pushed. Colin thought it was an accident and he protected the murderer. He didn't realise, you see, and the murderer was a patient of his – and a friend.

He thought he was just saving them distress, but actually he was covering up for them.'

'That's terrible,' Freda said.

'A terrible thing to do. Yes.'

'No, I meant terrible for him – to think he was doing something kind and then to find that he had just been used – by a friend.'

Eve looked at her. 'I can't think why we didn't tell you before,' she said.

They had reached the end of the garden and turned to come back.

'But how was Granny involved? Why was it her fault that Colin was in trouble?'

'She worked out who the murderer was and told the police. So then, of course, Colin was charged with obstructing their investigation.' She looked at Freda. 'Do you know, it's only when I tell it to you now that I see that I had no right to blame her? Of course she had to tell the police. The killer couldn't have been allowed to get away with it just to save Colin's skin – and he had been very foolish.'

Freda considered this. 'Granny can be quite annoying,' she said. 'I don't suppose she said she was sorry or anything. She'll have been a bit morally righteous, I expect.'

Eve put an arm round her and laughed. '*Morally righteous* – I couldn't have put it better,' she said. 'But we do love her, don't we?'

Back in the house, Freda looked into the sitting room, where her grandmother was sitting with Flossie, and without quite knowing why, she suddenly felt exasperated at the sight of her, looking as though she was posing, playing the role of a granny in a play, with her glasses on and her knitting that she was making such a fuss about. It was all fake, the anger in her head told her – she wasn't a sweet little granny at all, but a meddling know-all who went around messing up people's lives. She shut the door behind her and said, 'I've just really upset Colin and it's all your fault.'

Her grandmother reacted slowly, as though her mind had been somewhere far away. She put down her knitting, took off her glasses and said, 'What are you talking about, Freda?'

Freda went closer, so she could talk quietly. 'I'm talking about Colin and what happened in Marlbury with that girl and how you went to the police and never told me because you were ashamed of yourself and I talked to him about Amy Robsart and he's really upset and I wish I could just go home.'

Her grandmother sat looking at her. *Apologise!* Freda thought. *Why can't you just apologise?*

'Well, if I'd known you were doing your project on Amy Robsart,' she said, 'of course I would have warned you about talking to Colin. But as you decided to make it a secret – well, that's what happens with secrets.'

'I didn't tell you because you would have taken it over,' Freda shouted, too angry now to care whether anyone heard her. 'It would have become your project, not mine, because that's what you always do.'

Her grandmother picked up her knitting again. 'Well, there it is,' she said. 'I seem to remember that one of the reasons why you wanted to spend the lockdown with me was so that I could help with school work, but if you'd rather go to Colin for advice on Elizabethan England, feel free.'

'You are just the most annoying person!' Freda said, and slammed out of the room.

Out in the hall, she didn't know what to do with herself. At home, if she and her mum had a row, she would go out for a walk, but if she tried to do that here, Granny would probably come trailing behind her, like she did on the morning walks. She would just have to go up to her room, but it was so small and she was so angry that she felt as though she would end up beating her head against the wall. Starting to walk up the stairs, she saw that the door of Colin's study was open and he was sitting at his desk with his tea. On an impulse, she turned back and tapped on the open door. She had no idea what she was going to say but she had to say something. What came out surprised her.

'I just wanted to say I'm sorry I scared you on the stairs,' she said. 'You and Eve are the kindest people I know and I wouldn't want to do anything to upset you. That's all.'

And before he could answer she turned and ran up the stairs.

Chapter Sixteen

SOCIAL BUBBLE

May 5th

Well, it was bound to happen. Lock up any group of people together for weeks on end in anxious times and at least two of them will have a fight eventually. Unless they are nuns, possibly. And in our case, one of the two was always going to be me, wasn't it? I don't know, of course, what goes on in private between Eve and Colin, but they seem to have a pretty harmonious way of going on, and Freda was never going to have a row with either of them since she thinks they are perfect, so that leaves me having a row with any or all of the three of them. Not Eve; we know each other too well now and Eve is very good at heading off possible conflict. It might have been Colin; we are both having to make quite an effort not to clash, I think, because we both like being in charge. As it is, it turns out to be Freda. Would we have rowed if we had been together in my flat? Probably. And I attempt to console myself for the misery I feel with the conviction that, in this case at least, Freda is entirely in the wrong. Colin did a wrong and foolish thing ten years ago and Eve didn't want her grandsons, and therefore Freda, who is their friend, to know about it. Freda, for reasons of her own, made a secret of the topic of her History project. Result: she blunders into a conversation with Colin about a young woman being killed by a fall down some stairs, and he is upset. How is any of this my fault?

I am reminded of a conversation I had with Annie once, when she was fourteen or fifteen. She was at her most difficult – rude and uncooperative at school, stroppy and disruptive at home – and I was dealing with it alone, Andrew having lost interest entirely. She sang in the school choir, when she bothered to turn up to practices, and she was involved in a prestige event at which the choir of her posh school (the one thing Andrew did do, against my better judgement, was pay school fees) joined forces with the choirs of two posh local boarding schools to give a concert. Annie came home from this day out as high as a kite and full of talk about what a great time the other kids had at their schools, and for a moment I glimpsed salvation. Would she like to go to boarding school? Andrew would pay, I felt sure. A break for both of us and she would come back for the holidays newly appreciative of home and of me. And in term time there would be peace – just Ellie and me and the cat. No daily morning battle to drag her out of bed, no arguments over the contents of packed lunches, no pressure over homework undone, no fights about her going *just out*. In my most reasonable tone I asked, 'Do you think you might like to go to one of those schools? Better than St Margaret's? We could think about it.'

She was startled but I could see she was thinking about it. Then she said, 'No. It might be fun, but what would you do when you wanted to shout at someone?'

So there it was. The world was not as she would like it to be, and though she couldn't hold me responsible for all of it, it was my role to be shouted at. And that's how it was with Freda yesterday, I think, and she is going to have to mend this because I am not going to apologise for being a punching bag. She can just sit on the naughty step and think about what she has done wrong.

All of which doesn't stop me from feeling wretched as she and I edge round each other, coolly civil and uncomfortably distant. Eve must have noticed, I'm sure, and must know the reason. I hope she feels guilty. To make matters worse, when we are back from the morning walk and I turn on my laptop, I find an alarming message from the authorities at work: the Chinese government's surveillance apparatus is hacking into Zoom webinars and other such online platforms to monitor for any criticism of the government from Chinese students. I am urged to make sure that my students understand this and adjust their contributions accordingly. Reading this, I feel stupid that I hadn't thought of it before, alarmed about what I know has already been said in the students' mock presentations, and then overwhelmingly depressed at the knowledge – not new – that there will always be people for whom a bad situation is simply an opportunity to make things worse.

I pace around my little bedroom as though it were a prison cell. I need to talk to someone, and it can't be Eve because I am too cross with her. I consider Ellie or Annie but I spoke to both of them only a few days ago and I don't want to seem needy. David? Well, he is in the throes of a high-profile murder inquiry so of course, there is nothing he would like less than to listen to me rant on about freedom of speech and state terrorism. What he might do is give me some crumb of information about the case, though – just enough to distract me from my miseries and give me grist for milling. I get out my phone, and there, as though sent to me by a wish-granting genie, I find a remarkable update.

My phone and I don't understand each other. I know how to use it: I can make calls, send texts and emails, order groceries, check the weather forecast, take photos and even listen to audiobooks. I understand that what I have in my hand is a miniature computer but I don't, of course, understand how it works, and in particular I don't understand how it selects what news updates to send me. Because it clearly doesn't understand me. It seems to think that I have a passionate interest in the most trivial aspects of the lives of our royal family – not just the main players but the whole lot, right down to the York princesses and the Countess of Wessex. Nothing could be further from the truth, and I am not that interested in David Tennant either. He's a gifted actor but I really don't need regular updates on his domestic life. What I would like to know is whether I have brought this stuff on myself. Have I, in some forgotten moment, googled Tennant or Eugenie? Are cookies at work here? I really don't think so, but we don't all get the same updates – I've checked, and some people get better ones than mine. Mine almost all come from the red top papers, and I can only think that they have some kind of deal with Samsung. This morning, however, all is forgiven, because I am presented with a treasure.

What I have here – procured by bribery and corruption, without doubt – are text messages sent to Rebecca Clarke shortly before she was murdered. The accompanying news burble doesn't name the sender 'for legal reasons', as though illegality was a problem for them, but the clear implication is that the police believe the sender to be the killer. However, it is very possible that this is a hoax. There is only one way to find out.

'Scott.'

Why do I so like the way he answers his phone?

'Gray,' I say.

'Gina.'

'Busy?'

'You could say.'

'I won't keep you. Just tell me, hoax or not?'

A hesitation. 'Not.'

'The official line?'

'No comment.'

'Heads will roll?'

'As we speak.'

'Well, it's brightened my day.'

He rings off.

I make a cup of coffee, collect a chocolate biscuit and settle down to study the texts as though they were a new Rosetta stone. Sadly, they are pretty underwhelming. There are only two of them and they are very short:

dont think you can cansel me bich think your so grate just wait; you got it cumming stuckup cow ingoring me im cumming for you.

It doesn't take a linguistic expert to conclude that the intent is to threaten and the sender is semi-literate. Beyond that, what can my expert eye discern? Well, very little really. The errors are what you would expect: no apostrophes or other punctuation, no capitals, phonetic spelling of *coming* and *great*, c/s confusion in *cancel*, and letter transposition in *ignoring* to the more familiar *ing*. Nothing surprising, and yet they bother me. Something doesn't feel right but I don't know what it is, and I should know. If things were normal, if I were at my desk at work, if Freda wasn't judging me, if I hadn't made a fool of myself over the neighbours, I would see these things clearly, identify the problem and be on the phone to David to make my crucial contribution to the case. As it is, I just sit and stare at my phone as my coffee cools and the chocolate biscuit makes me feel queasy.

The messages are pathetic, of course – angry and needy. Would a girl like Rebecca even have felt threatened? The teenage social world is nature in the raw and everyone knows their place from alphas to epsilons. This boy didn't stand a chance with her and must have known it. I was shocked by Freda, back last summer, when we were talking about *Twelfth Night,* and she said she had no sympathy for Malvolio because Olivia was obviously out of his league and he ought to know it. She was quite matter-of-fact about it – that was simply how the world was. So why did this illiterate boy feel that he had a right to respect? It is odd and my brain feels flaccid and unhelpful.

I go downstairs with my knitting. The usual pattern of my day is that I work in the mornings, after the walk; answering emails, tweaking lecture notes for next term, reading any bits of dissertation that my students have sent me. If there is not much of that to do then I read an improving book – Jenny Offill's *Weather* at the moment – not comfortable reading but exhilarating, I find. Then, after lunch, I settle down with the knitting. It is actually going rather well. There was a lot of yellow and orange wool in Eve's bag, so my design is somewhere between a sunburst and a sunflower, with an orange centre and shading out to green and blue round the edges. Nine days in, I have done six squares, but I am approaching Eve's target of one a day, and I do find it quite satisfying. I can sit and think, and in the late afternoon there are often good programmes on the radio. Today though, I am punishing myself. If I am going to be stupid then I might as well sit and knit like the old granny that I am, and sitting here reminds me that Eve started me on this as a punishment, however sweetly she sugar-coated it. I was stupid over Paul and Elise and I had to be kept out of mischief. In fact, I am the one on the naughty step. I wish I could go home.

Chapter Seventeen

SAVE LIVES

May 6th

It was quite disappointing to see how Robert Dudley reacted to the news that his wife had died. Freda really had wanted to believe that he loved Amy and was kept apart from her only because he couldn't offend the queen, but when she looked at the letter he wrote when he first got the news, she had to say that the only person Lord Robert loved was himself. He started by talking about *the greatness and suddenness of the misfortune,* which seemed promising, but then he went straight on to *the malicious talk that I know the wicked world will use,* and that was obviously what he really cared about. Amy's death was too convenient and it fitted too well with the rumours going around that he and the queen were trying to get rid of her. Freda could see that Robert was in a scary situation. They had done a bit in History at school about how news got around Tudor England – town criers for the official news, and pamphlets and ballads for the sort of stuff that went around social media now. There was quite a lot in Christine Hartweg's book about the rumours that were spread around about Robert. And he would have known that the pamphlet-writers and ballad-makers were going to go into overdrive. But just a word of grief for his wife would have been nice, she thought.

What did seem to be clear, though, was that he hadn't organised or ordered her killing – not unless he was an excellent liar, which she supposed he might have been. What he did when he got the news was to write to his steward, Sir Walter Blount, who was also his cousin, and give him detailed instructions about finding out the truth of what had happened – *whether by evil chance or by villainy*. So it was really down to him that there was such a detailed coroner's report, because he instructed Sir Walter to tell the coroner that he was to have *no light or slight persons* on the coroner's jury to examine the body, but *the discreetest and most substantial men, who would be able to search thoroughly and duly by all manner of examinations the bottom of the matter*. What he also said – and this was really interesting – was that Sir Walter was to *use all the devices and means possible for the learning of the truth, wherein have no respect to any living person*. In other words, it looked as though Robert thought that the person responsible might be someone Sir Walter might be afraid of naming. Who was he thinking of? Not the queen, surely, because no-one would have dared to name her. So who?

It was all very interesting, and she was trying to get absorbed in it so that she didn't have to think about what had happened with Granny yesterday. She couldn't remember now exactly why she had been so angry with her. It had been Eve's and Colin's secret after all. She had been angry with herself, really, for upsetting Colin, and she supposed she should have been angry with Eve but she didn't want to be, so she had been angry with Granny instead. And then Granny had been annoying – being so sort of *calm*, so that Freda felt like a baby having a tantrum when she shouted at her. But now she knew she should be the one to apologise really, and she couldn't find a way of doing it – not when Granny was being all distant and polite and making her want to yell at her all over again.

Supper that evening was risotto, which Granny had made, and nearly the whole conversation as they were eating it was about the risotto itself – how delicious Colin's asparagus was, how much better the homemade vegetable stock was than anything you got from a cube, how you had to use proper risotto rice and it was worth the trouble to stand over it, ladling in the stock bit by bit. It was a nice risotto, but really it was just rice with vegetables in it and Freda thought this was the most boring conversation they had ever had. Usually supper-time talk was lively. Everyone reported on their doings of the day and what they had read in or heard on the news, and they discussed and argued and joked. She looked forward to it, but tonight it was just dull. It was her fault. It was obvious that she and Granny weren't really speaking to each other, so everyone was avoiding subjects that might start an argument. And you couldn't argue about vegetables, could you?

When they had finished, Eve volunteered for the washing up and shooed Freda away when she offered to help. Colin went off to his study and Granny went into the sitting room, back to her precious knitting. Nothing had been said about TV plans for the evening and Freda had no intention of just going in and sitting with her there. On the other hand, she didn't want to go up to her room either because she had been there most of the day and she felt too restless to settle down with a book up there. Standing in the hall, at a loss about where to go, she saw Flossie's lead hanging over the stair post and made a snap decision. Pulling her jacket off its peg, she picked up the lead and went to find Flossie, who would, she knew, be in the kitchen hoping for scraps, though she was out of luck after a vegetarian supper.

Calculating on taking Eve by surprise, she said breezily, 'All right with you if I just take Flossie for a run round the block? I need to get out and clear my head.'

Flossie was on her side, the appearance of the lead sending her into an ecstasy of tail-wagging and leaping into the air. Eve glanced at her and then out of the window. 'Well, it's still light and I don't mind, but you ought to ask Granny.'

'She won't mind,' Freda said, fastening the lead, and then sped out of the room in time to be able to claim that she didn't hear Eve say, 'Ask her anyway'. She picked up her phone from the hall table and went out, closing the door behind her as quietly as possible.

Outside the house, she decided not to turn towards the lake, as that was the route they took every morning, but to turn the other way. *Round the block* was just an expression really, but that was basically where she would go, with no chance of getting lost. She looked at her watch. Ten or fifteen minutes was all she needed. Granny couldn't get into a state in that time, could she?

It was weirdly quiet – there were still very few cars around and most people were indoors beginning their evenings. Although it was technically still light and the sun hadn't gone down, it was overcast and gloomy, with the kind of fine drizzle in the air that there was most of the time up here – mizzle, they called it – and as she waited for Flossie to sniff around and have a pee, she thought about how Granny liked to list the words that there were in English for different kinds of rain. She ran through them for herself as she set off to walk into eerie silence: *mizzle* and *drizzle* and *spits and spots, a scotch mist* and *an April shower, teeming, pouring, drenching* and *bucketing, cats and dogs* and *nice weather for ducks.* It was comforting somehow. And she had Flossie, and Flossie was finding interest in every blade of grass along the verge. She turned right at the end of the road and as she started up the unfamiliar street, she thought she could hear footsteps echoing in the silence, approaching the corner. Speeding up, she tugged Flossie away from an exciting lamp post. The steps turned the corner and started up behind her. She was determined not to turn round or look nervous, and there was no point in trying to hurry because if her follower was out to get her, he would be able to run faster than her, wouldn't he? She stopped while Flossie crouched for a poo, registering that she had forgotten to bring poo bags, but too bad, and listening all the time. It seemed to her that the footsteps had stopped. If someone was following her, they weren't trying to catch up with her. Were they just trying to scare her?

'OK, Flossie, let's go,' she said, more loudly than she needed to, and her voice echoed among the silent houses, where curtains were starting to be drawn. She urged Flossie on, up the road and round the next corner. The footsteps behind her started up again. Walking more briskly, she looked at the windows of houses as she passed them, with an eye out for signs of life and a possible refuge if she needed it, and then, outside a house with a van in its drive, she stood and stared. In the lit window were a man and a woman, and he had his hands round her throat. Her brain raced around for explanations – they were just messing around, they were rehearsing a scene in a play – but there was no mistaking the fury in his face or the terror in hers. And she recognised the man; he was the creepy guy who used to watch them from under the trees on their morning walks.

She dug in her pocket for her phone and, with a sense of total unreality, dialled 999. At the same moment, a figure barged past her, ran up the drive and banged furiously on the window, shouting, 'Leave her alone, you bastard. Leave her alone.' It was, of course, Granny.

As she was registering this, Flossie started barking and a voice was saying, 'Emergency. Which service do you require?' and she was controlling the wobble in her voice enough to say, 'Police – and ambulance, I think. There's a woman being attacked.'

Her eyes were still fixed on the window and she saw the man give the woman a hard shove that sent her out of sight, and then come to the window, literally snarling at Granny, who shouted over her shoulder to Freda, 'Seventeen Bramley Road,' before turning back to confront the snarling man and shouting, 'The police are on their way,' at him before he pulled the curtains closed. Freda gave the address to the woman on the phone and Granny gave the window a final bang and came back to the pavement.

'Well done,' she said.

'Why were you following me?'

'*Never out of my sight.* I promised your mum.'

Then the front door of the house opened and Granny wrapped her in a protective hug while Flossie started up a barrage of barking, but the person who came out was the woman, barefoot and wearing pyjamas. Granny squeezed past the van and up the drive just in time to catch her as she collapsed to the ground, dropping the bunch of keys she was carrying. Picking up the keys, Granny pulled the front door closed and turned the key in the lock. Then she returned to the woman, took her own jacket off and wrapped it round her, and helped her carefully to her feet. Half carrying her, she brought her to where Freda was standing, with Flossie now silent beside her. She sat her down on the low front wall, sat beside her and took off her own shoes and socks. 'My shoes will be too big,' she said, 'but have the socks.' The woman shook her head and then seemed to fold up in the middle, bending her head to her knees so Freda could see clearly the red and purple marks around the back of her neck. She handed Flossie's lead to Granny, took the socks from her and knelt down to put the socks on the woman's icy feet.

'This is Elise,' Granny said. 'You may have seen her in her garden. It backs on to ours.'

Elise looked up and for a moment a flicker of interest

showed in her face. 'With Eve?' she croaked, her voice just a rattly whisper.

'Yes. I'm Gina. And this is my granddaughter, Freda.'

Freda and Elise looked at each other. *What were you supposed to say?* Freda wondered. *Pleased to meet you* didn't really cut it. But she need not have worried because Granny was still talking.

'Freda did exactly the right thing, and an ambulance will be here any minute.'

Elise seemed to shrink inside Granny's jacket, which was too big for her anyway. 'Not police?' she whispered.

'I'm afraid so,' Granny said, and then added, 'But I think they'll take you to hospital before they ask you any questions – and I shall come with you.'

Did she realise that Colin would make her isolate again? Freda wondered. She wouldn't care anyway, would she? And she suddenly felt such a burst of love for this bossy, loving, infuriating grandmother that she got up off her knees and dropped a kiss on the top of her head, just as a siren wailed and lights swept round the corner, just exactly as if they were on TV.

Chapter Eighteen

DAILY BRIEFING

May 7ᵗʰ

'And of course, I'm not glad that I was right. At one level I feel gutted to think of what has been going on almost literally on our doorstep, but I can't help feeling clearer somehow, not doubting myself.'

David Scott had put his phone on speaker and was scanning an update from Tom Ireland. He knew Gina well enough to be confident that she was not ringing just to triumph in her rescue or her rightness. There would be a point to all this, and he thought he could probably urge her towards it now. He picked up his phone.

'Doubting yourself?' he said. 'You?'

'Well, I did, and don't sound so surprised. I thought I'd made a fool of myself – and then there was Freda... but never mind all that. The point is that I am myself again and I've taken another look at those texts and I've seen that, of course, they're fake.'

'Fake in what sense?'

'Fake in the sense that the sender purports to be illiterate but isn't. And I'll tell you why – and I would have seen it before if I hadn't been so befuddled by the other stuff because it's really quite —'

'Hold on a minute,' he interrupted. 'We tested them out.

We had the boy in and asked him to write down the words that are misspelled in the texts. In nearly every case he misspelled them in the same way.'

'Of course he did. The writer isn't a fool – he knows what sort of mistakes kids with literacy problems make. What did he spell differently?'

'Just the words without apostrophes, I think. He wrote them out in full – *do not* et cetera.'

'Yes, he'll have had it drummed into him that you don't use short forms when you're doing formal writing, and he'll have thought that writing for the police was pretty formal.'

'So why do you say the texts are fake?'

'Try typing those texts in your phone with all the errors and see what happens.'

He didn't need to actually do it; he sat back in his chair, stunned by realisation.

'It will autocorrect,' he said.

'It will. The writer would have had to override autocorrect to send a message with all those errors in it.'

'Why didn't we see that?'

'Because we don't make errors – or if we do have the odd typo, it corrects so fast we don't notice.'

He was silent, thinking. There was that other text, wasn't there?

'How does the boy – I assume it's a boy? – explain the texts?'

'He says he lost his phone, and there's been no further activity on it.'

'So it could have been stolen and then ditched.'

'It could. I'll be honest with you, Gina – and I don't know why I am trusting you – our instinct was that this boy isn't the killer, so what you've said about the texts is helpful, but the stolen phone theory doesn't work altogether because there's another text, sent weeks before, just before lockdown. He denies sending it but the phone was definitely in his possession then.'

'What did the text say?'

'I'll send it to you.'

'You've looked at the YouTube video that the family put out, I assume?'

'The team have.'

'I'm going to look at it again. Everyone who was close to her is on that video.'

'But not our main suspect.'

'Send me that text.'

After he rang off, he sent the text immediately, and then tried typing the later texts. He knew Gina would be right, and she was. Every error was corrected, though no punctuation apart from apostrophes was added. Even if they thought the boy was guilty, a defence lawyer would have a field day with this. *Have a field day?* Where did that come from? Why was it that a conversation with Gina could always set up this internal language monitor in his head, his very own autocorrect? Feeling absurd, he googled *have a field day* and found thoroughly unsatisfactory answers – plenty of examples of its use, which he didn't need, and unhelpfully vague suggestions of its origins in military manoeuvres *carried out in a field*. Why would you do that? He could only assume that these manoeuvres were designed to impress and terrify – like North Korea's parades of tanks.

Enough. He would pass on the insight about the texts to Tom Ireland. He would be glad of something because the inquiry was, frankly, stalled. Interviewing the other kids who collected phones that day had got them nowhere, the ex-boyfriend's alibi held up, nothing more had come from forensics, and follow-up on CCTV footage in the car park by the river had produced no leads. The killer had known what he or she was doing. Later, he would take a look himself at the family's YouTube video, as Gina suggested, but in the meantime he went back to the pile of reports on his desk, glad to turn his mind to something else.

Chapter Nineteen

INTENSIVE CARE

May 6th and 7th

It is not until the next morning that I really feel the effects of the unexpected drama of the evening before. At the time there is too much confusion and too many things to worry about. To start with, when the emergency services arrive – blessedly soon, I must say – the paramedics won't let me go with Elise, COVID rules forbidding non-combatants to hang around in hospitals, and when I try to argue, the police officers chip in on their side and even they don't want us hanging around, so we just give our details and I hand over the house keys and we get shooed away without even having the satisfaction of seeing Paul Jessop brought out of the house. We do look over our shoulders as we go back down the road, and we see the ambulance drive away and the police go into the house, and we hang around on the corner for a bit, but nothing more happens.

'I did want to see him come out in handcuffs,' Freda says.

And so did I, but now I have other things to worry about as we walk the rest of the way home. First, there is Freda herself. What she saw was traumatic (I feel that the scene is burnt onto my retinas like an endlessly running clip from *Rear Window*) and once the euphoria of saving the day starts to wear off, who knows how she will feel? Then there is Eve.

I decide to let Freda tell her what has happened so that I don't seem to be crowing over being right about Paul Jessop, but she is going to feel terrible – worried about Elise, hurt that Elise hasn't been honest with her about what has been going on, and maybe a bit mortified about having told me off. And that's going to make it difficult for me to be any help. But what looms largest among my worries is that I shall have to tell Ellie. If I don't tell her she will find out. Freda can't be expected to keep this secret, and if (and I know it's a big *if*) there is a prosecution, then Freda will be a witness. Well, I never let her out of my sight, did I?

What follows is a difficult evening. When I say that there has been a bit of a drama, Colin disappears into his study and Freda takes Eve into the kitchen, while I go upstairs and phone Ellie, who quite unfairly demands to know why I am a magnet for trouble and says she wants Freda home just as soon as travel restrictions are lifted. I ring off feeling hard done by and go downstairs to make sure that Freda is all right and to suggest hot chocolate all round as a general mood-enhancer. Eve is crying in the kitchen but repels all my attempts at comfort, including the hot chocolate. Then, as I am carrying mugs upstairs for Freda and me, Colin comes bursting out of his study, definitely the worse for drink and demanding to know whether this drama of ours had involved us getting close to anyone. Thoroughly rattled, I reply that another two weeks of isolation would suit me just fine at the moment but that the only person we had been close to was a woman who had been subject to draconian shielding, that the paramedics had been covered in PPE, and that the police officers shouted at us from the obligatory two-metre distance.

'I don't expect you to believe me,' I end up saying, 'but if you want to check with Freda, you are not to do it now. You can leave it to the morning – when you're sober.'

Then I storm up the stairs, insofar as one can *storm* with a mug of hot chocolate in each hand.

But this morning I do feel better. I'm still worried about them all – Elise, Freda, Eve – but I can't help that quickening of the blood, the little boost of adrenaline, probably, that tells me that I am not a fool and that self-doubt is not an option. So it is this new bounce that sends me back to those text messages, which have been bugging me since I first read them, because I know I have been being stupid about them. Of course I have. As soon as I see them again, I know what is wrong with them, and I can't wait to get on the phone to David. He may have disdained my claims to special expertise in the language of teenage girls, but illiterate teenage boys I do know.

So now he has sent me the other text – the one the boy sent earlier, and I can see immediately what has happened here. It is very short: *Sorry about tongue and been a pest hope we are friends.*

He has added a smiley face. It is quite different from the later messages – autocorrected (perhaps excessively) and not threatening in tone at all – but I suppose *tongue* and *pest* sound alarms for people who are listening for them. *Pest* I think we don't have to worry about. Of course there are sex pests, but they don't know that they are pests, do they? Or if they do know, they certainly don't admit that their behaviour is pestiferous. *Just being friendly,* they say, *just a bit of fun, harmless flirting*. So if there is a problem it's the tongue, for which the boy apologises. This does suggest inappropriate behaviour, and possibly sexual harassment, though is there a girl or woman in this country who has not had a male tongue thrust uninvited into her mouth at some time? When I was doing student theatre, I was quite certain that most of the men only joined a drama group because it gave them the opportunity for that sort of thing.

Anyway, I think I know where the *tongue* comes from in this message. It is a very odd message when you look at it. *Sorry about tongue.* The boy may have literacy problems but he's not a non-native speaker. Why not at least *the tongue* or *my tongue*, or even *the stuff with the tongue*? So maybe he wasn't intending to write tongue at all. I try the message out on my phone.

Sorry about, and then he wants to write a word that doesn't need an article in front of it. If he didn't mean *tongue*, my guess is that he was going for *tonight. Sorry about tonight* must be a fairly common message after all – *Sorry about today, Sorry about yesterday, Sorry about earlier* – we have all sent them. But the boy's problem is that he doesn't know how to spell *tonight.* His instinct would be to spell it phonetically – *tonite* – but he knows that's wrong. *Night* has a *'g'* in it, he's pretty sure, so he tries *tong,* and bingo, up springs *tongue.* He has no idea how you spell the thing in your mouth, and he certainly wouldn't expect it to be spelt like that, so he accepts *tongue* for *tonight* and sends his message. And of course he denied sending that message when the police questioned him, because that wasn't the message he thought he had sent.

I send a text myself to David, explaining succinctly my line of reasoning. *Ask the boy if he sent a message saying 'Sorry about tonight',* I conclude, and sit back, wondering what the lad had actually been apologising for. Just hanging around and being in the way, probably. I remember how insistent the girls were on the video about Rebecca's kindness to everyone, even to people that others laughed at. Perhaps he had tested even her kindness too far.

I don't know who he is, of course, but I don't remember any boys on the family's video except the ex-boyfriend, who was articulate and confident – definitely not this boy. I get myself a cup of coffee and settle down to watch the video again.

139

The early part is not going to offer me any clues, I think, though that doesn't mean that I don't shed tears over the sunny childhood clips. Any childhood can be given the gloss of happiness in retrospect with the aid of some creative cutting and splicing, but I get the feeling that Rebecca Clarke was blessed with love and security, and there has been no suggestion in any of the media reporting, or in my terse conversations with David, that her family are suspects in her killing. Then I watch her friends, struggling to find the vocabulary to particularise the girl they loved, having to resort to the banal – *she was really kind, she never made anyone feel bad, she was so brilliant* – but making the trite phrases meaningful through the earnestness of their gaze and the shakiness in their voices. I look again at her sister. It isn't easy to be the sister of a star. Could she have hated Rebecca at times? Probably. I was an only child so I haven't experinced sibling love and hate myself, but I saw plenty of it in my daughters as they angled and pushed for their place in the pecking order at their highly competitive school. I never thought there was any danger of their killing one another though. So I move on, through the tributes from the teachers – the head and the deputy head, with their contrasting styles, home interiors and supporting wives. When the choir arrives I switch off. I have wept enough for one morning.

There is the faintest of alarm bells in my mind, like a false note I know has just been played but I can't remember the phrase well enough to say what it was. I could watch the video again but I'm afraid repetition might make me deaf. I decide to leave it and let my mind settle. In the meantime, I shall check up on the rest of the household.

I have seen Freda already this morning; we ate breakfast together and then did the dog walk. The girls have taken to ending the walk by sitting on adjacent benches in the town square for a high-volume exchange of news and views, and this morning, of course, Freda had to unburden herself of the events of last night. It was early and no-one else was in the square but I was still uncomfortable about a domestic tragedy being broadcast in this way, and I didn't want to be part of it, so I opted for prowling around them, with Flossie, but Grace and Ruby, who experienced their own share of abuse in the past, were rivetted by her narrative.

'But I do wish I could have seen him taken away in handcuffs,' Freda said eventually, and the girls sat with faraway gazes, contemplating the pure satisfaction of that image. Now I put my head round her door and find her busy typing. 'Just coming to the end of my project,' she says, without turning round. 'I'm going to be just in the word limit.'

'What's the limit?'

'Two thousand five hundred words.'

'Will I be allowed to read it?'

'Certainly. After I've sent it in.'

When it's too late for me to make helpful suggestions for improvements. 'I'm looking forward to it,' I say.

Then I go downstairs to check on Eve, whom I haven't yet seen this morning, and Colin, whom I don't much want to see. I don't intend to apologise for commenting on his drinking; Eve and I have pussyfooted around for too long about Colin's two-bottle evening habits and the boxes that get delivered from the off-licence. And I was quite right to warn him off cross-questioning Freda when she had been through an alarming experience and he was the worse for wear. But he is my host and I don't suppose he sees it like that.

I find Eve in her shed. She is sitting on a stool, painting a pot in a bright turquoise, very unlike the subtle, misty colours she generally uses these days.

'Jolly, isn't it?' she says dismissively, reading my thoughts. 'Time for jollying up the tourists with shouty colours.'

I find a packing case to sit on. 'Have you heard from Elise?' I ask.

'What?' She purports to be concentrating fiercely on this simple painting job. 'Oh, no. But they have rules about phones in hospitals, don't they?'

'I'm thinking she probably doesn't have her phone with her. She was in her pyjamas and she just ran out. She was —'

'Yes, I heard. You don't need to tell me again.' She puts down her brush. 'Is there something I can do for you, Gina?'

This is another version of *Can I help you?*, of course.

'I'm sorry Elise didn't tell you what was going on,' I say.

'Yes, well.' She gets up and starts rearranging some pots on a shelf, so that she has her back to me. 'I didn't know her really. They haven't been here long. We bonded a bit over shielding, but you don't just come out and say, *Oh, by the way, my husband has me locked up here and he's violent and I'm afraid of him.*'

'You might, if you wanted help.'

'But I couldn't have helped, could I?' Now she turns round. 'I'm in the same boat. Locked up, I mean.'

'But you're not afraid of Colin.'

'No, of course not. But what could I have done if she'd told me? Tell the police? He's very plausible. I was taken in. All his concern about her and not daring to leave her alone.'

'It might have helped her at least to talk about it.'

'How? I'd have started telling her what she should do about it and she knew she couldn't do any of it.'

'Well, I'm sorry anyway,' I say and I get up. 'Shall I make pancakes for lunch? We can have them as follow-up to your *zuppa verde.*'

She gives a little bark of a laugh. 'You are the most improbable earth mother,' she says, 'but you do think anything can be made better by food and drink, don't you? Hot chocolate and pancakes and all manner of things shall be well.'

'Dame Julian of Norwich,' I say. 'All most of us know about her is *All shall be well and all shall be well and all manner of things shall be well.* I heard an interesting radio programme about her once, where an academic was claiming that that statement was a deliberate challenge to the male authority of the church, which was constantly telling people that they would end up in hell fire and all would be far from well.'

'I don't suppose she put her faith in pancakes, though.'

I am not offended. I know she's right about my urge to feed people. 'OK then, I won't,' I say in a mock huff. 'We'll just drink your measly soup, which gives me the runs, by the way.'

'Me too. Make the pancakes.'

My phone is ringing when I get back into the house and I hare upstairs to catch it just in time. It is DC Mark Abington. 'We weren't expecting to be seeing you again, Mrs Gray,' he says.

Is this a good start? The last time I had dealings with the Carnmere police was last summer, and then I was a bit of a heroine, but my reappearance may make them suspect me of looking for trouble. (What, *moi*?) I try getting ahead of him.

'It does rather look as though trouble follows me around, doesn't it? Even in lockdown,' I say.

'It does,' he says, and I don't hear him smiling. 'We'd like to come and talk to you and your granddaughter this afternoon. I assume that you're not going anywhere?'

I then have to explain about Eve's shielding and the impossibility of having anyone in the house. 'I suppose we could talk in the garden,' I say, 'but we would have to shout at each other from two metres apart, which hardly feels right for a sensitive issue like this. Or we could just talk on the phone, of course.'

I am annoying him, making suggestions when it is my place to do as I'm told. He says he will ring me back and returns, after consultation – possibly with DS Hapgood, who also interviewed me last summer – to say that they will talk to us online and we will have a link emailed to us.

'Will you be able to do that?' he asks.

Riled at the implication that I am too old or stupid to manage online meetings, I start to tell him that I have recently not just joined but set up international Zoom meetings, but he cuts me short.

'We shall need to talk to you and your granddaughter separately,' he says.

I insist that I must be present at Freda's interview in *loco parentis*. He says they will talk to me first and then I can join their meeting with Freda, and rings off.

I go in to give Freda the news. 'We don't need to worry about getting our stories straight,' I say. 'We'll both just tell it as we saw it. There is just one thing, though. Do you think we can say that we were out walking Flossie together? If we say that I was following you, it might seem a bit weird.'

'It was weird.'

'I know. But we don't want them to think that we're so weird that they can't believe us.'

'OK,' she says. 'I fudged the truth when they interviewed me last year, so I expect I can do it again.'

'I'm making pancakes for lunch,' I say, and go downstairs.

Chapter Twenty

WEAR A MASK

May 8th

As easy as lying. She had remembered that line from when they had watched *Hamlet.* It was the bit with the recorders, when Hamlet was talking to his friends and told them he knew they were lying to him. She had noticed it because she didn't find lying easy. She was bad at it. She went red and couldn't look people in the eye. Even Nico knew when she wasn't telling him the truth. So she avoided lying whenever possible. It felt easier that way. The lie to the police yesterday had seemed as though it would be such a small thing, though: *Granny and I were taking the dog for an evening walk.* How could that be a problem? And yet it was. Somehow, DC Abington seemed to be obsessed by their reasons for the walk. *Did they always walk the dog at that time? Was it always she and her grandmother who did it? No? Why that evening then? Did they always walk along that road when they went out? No? Why that evening then?* She realised after a bit that what he was suspicious about was whether they had really just gone out for a walk and happened to be walking past when Elise was attacked. It probably didn't help that he remembered them from last summer, because it would seem too much of a coincidence to him that they had got themselves mixed up in a crime twice. From the way he questioned her, she could see that he suspected that they were spying on the house. He asked whether she had ever seen the couple before, and when she said that she had noticed the man hanging around in the mornings he got very interested in that. She felt uncomfortable that she hadn't been completely honest. Now her lie, small though it was, was a *fact*. It was written diwn in her statement and she had signed it, No wonder you could never know what had actually happened. No wonder history was so slippery.

Afterwards Granny had needed to do a lot of venting to anyone who would listen about the way the police dealt with domestic violence. *They could see the marks on her neck*, she kept saying. *And how is this kind of abuse going to come to light if people don't report it? If they make people feel like liars when they report things then they're colluding with the abusers.* Freda had listened for a bit but she was just glad that it was over and she wanted to get back to her project because she was at the point of polishing up the conclusion. Then she would email it to Mrs Yardley and that would be it. Done. As soon as she could, she slipped away – back to the 16th century.

Now, this morning, she was sitting at her desk, rereading her conclusion:

When Amy Robsart became Amy Dudley just before her 18th birthday, it must have seemed to her like a teenage girl's dream come true. She was marrying the man she had fallen in love with, and though he was not quite a prince, he was a handsome young aristocrat from one of England's most powerful families. Both families were happy with the marriage and the King of England was at her wedding.

For the first year, things went well. Her husband became a Member of Parliament, they were given a house to live in by his father, and they had relatives in London who they could stay with when they wanted more excitement.

A year after the wedding, Robert's father was made Duke of Northumberland, making Robert 'Lord Robert' and his wife 'Lady Amy'. Lord Robert had a place at court and their future must have looked very bright.

Then disaster fell on the family. King Edward VI died, Robert's father attempted to seize the throne for Lady Jane Grey, his son Guildford's wife, and all the Dudleys were arrested and imprisoned in the Tower of London. From being a courtier's wife, Amy found herself visiting her husband in jail. Robert's father was convicted of treason and executed, and all the family lands and money were confiscated by the Crown. Robert was lucky to escape with his life, but he and Amy were in disgrace and penniless, depending on handouts from Amy's family.

Robert had to start again, to try to build up a career as a courtier, and he did this by fighting for the queen in France. As a result, he and Amy never really lived together again. Amy's life was very different from what she may have imagined when she married, and she had no children to occupy her. When Queen Mary died and Princess Elizabeth became queen, she immediately summoned Robert to court and in no time everyone was talking about him as the queen's favourite and speculating about a marriage.

It is not possible to know how Amy felt about this new situation, and that is why it is so difficult to come to a conclusion about her death. She had shown herself to be strong. She survived the ups and downs of the family's fortunes and managed her husband's practical affairs while he was away fighting or at court, but knowing that her life was all that stood between her husband and marrying the queen must have been extremely difficult. And she does not seem to have had anyone to confide in. She had no sisters and her mother was dead. Robert arranged for her to live with different people who were loyal to his family, so that she would have company, but they were not her friends. In that situation, it would not be surprising if she became depressed and suicidal, but she had a strong religious faith and the Church ruled that suicide was a sin, so I have been inclined to rule out suicide.

Her death could have been an accident, as the coroner ruled. She had sent all her servants off to the fair. Perhaps if they had been there they would have lit candles and the staircase would not have been so dark. Also, she was staying in someone else's house, so was more likely to miss her footing in an unfamiliar place. An accident is the least interesting cause of her death though.

Was she murdered? If Amy was murdered, it was not by her husband, or on his orders, because as I showed earlier, when the news of her death reached him, he saw at once that this was a disaster for him because suspicion would fall on him and he would be in disgrace with the queen. It might have seemed that killing Amy off would free him to marry the queen, but actually it was the one thing that would make it impossible because of the scandal. So if we are looking for the murderer, we have to look for someone who was desperate to stop the queen from marrying Robert, and my chosen culprit is William Cecil, Lord Burghley.

William Cecil and Lord Robert Dudley had been competing for influence over the queen from the start of her reign. Cecil, as her chief counsellor, offered her statecraft and cunning, while Lord Robert offered charm and flattery. If Cecil believed the rumours about Amy's ill-health then he must have feared that she would die of natural causes and the queen would marry Lord Robert, and his influence would be at an end. (To be fair, he may have been afraid that it would be bad for the country as well). Cecil was a cunning and devious man, and he may have seen that the *only way to make things safe was to have Amy die under mysterious circumstances that would throw suspicion on Lord Robert.*

Cecil probably did not send hired assassins from London to kill Amy because whoever killed her must have known the layout of the house well. They needed to know that Amy's apartments had their own staircase down to the house's central courtyard. They also needed to know that her servants would be out of the way. If modern police were investigating this death, I think they would be looking among the household servants (not Amy's own servants). Cecil may have bribed one of the servants, or even placed someone paid by him in the household. The killer could have been watching for an opportunity and taken advantage of Amy's servants going to the fair, or, as I suggested earlier, Amy might have sent her servants off because she was expecting a secret visit. From what I have read about Cecil, he could have sent a forged letter to Amy, pretending to be from her husband, arranging a visit.

I know this is speculation, and we shall never know the truth, but William Cecil had a strong motive and the power to find the means and opportunity. I name him as the guilty man.

It was, she thought, quite good. She ran the spellcheck once more, and then emailed it to Mrs Yardley. It was another week till the deadline, but she didn't want to be tinkering with it anymore. And Mrs Yardley might be more generous with her marking for the projects that arrived early, before she had a great pile of them and felt tired and grumpy. It was an advantage to have a mum who was a teacher because you knew the way their minds worked. She emailed the project to Colin with a request for printing and waited. A message came back immediately – *On it* – and another few minutes later – *Done*. She went downstairs to pick it up and liked the feel of it in her hands; it felt substantial, she thought.

Back upstairs she knocked on her grandmother's door, realising as she did so that she was cradling her project, holding it to her heart as though it was a baby. Hastily she took it between two fingers, so that as she walked into the room she could dangle it casually and say, 'Thought you might be interested in having a look at this some time.' She dropped it onto the bed and turned to leave, saying as she went, 'It's gone to Mrs Yardley now, so this is it.'

Back in her room she checked her emails – nothing interesting – and got out her Art project sketches. She could add another, she thought, now that the trees were in full blossom in the square. Would she still be here when the area was full of shoppers once again? Mum had phoned, all steamed up about them getting involved with the police again and saying that Nonna and Nonno were going home as soon as flying was allowed, and then she wanted her home. Freda had protested but there was a bit of her now that actually quite wanted that.

Chapter Twenty-One

TRACK AND TRACE

May 10th

Defying accusations of granny-boasting, I have to tell you that Freda's project is excellent. It is not perfect, of course; her tone is somewhat uncertain, swinging between striving for an 'academic' style and veering towards the conversational when she gets really engaged with her topic, and the logic of her argument isn't always watertight. A bit of advice from me would not have gone amiss, I think, though when I look at what I have just written I realise that my comments are probably less appropriate for a Year Nine project than they are for an MA dissertation.

The fact is that it is very good and it gets me thinking. Of course Freda has picked William Cecil for her villain; she has had it in for him ever since he started spying on the state of the queen's bedsheets. I don't know if there is any evidence that the real William Cecil did that, but it seems quite probable. They none of them knew what to do with a female monarch, did they? They had had Mary, of course, but there was King Philip as well, so Mary could still be seen as a wife and potential heir-bearer. Now they were faced with a young, single woman who had to be treated with all the deference due to a monarch but whom they could not help seeing as another royal female to be used to make marital alliances and increase the royal stock. Robert Cecil was a real complication – handsome enough to remind the queen that she was a young woman, and aristocratic and ambitious enough to set his sights on a throne of his own. And Dudley and Cecil were kids on a see-saw – when one was up, the other had to be down. Did Cecil decide to topple Robert Dudley off the see-saw altogether? He would have had no qualms about sacrificing Amy Dudley – women were an unreliable commodity after all, easily spoiled, their hold on life tenuous when every pregnancy was a potential death sentence. And when that happened, men just married again. Wives were disposable.

Disposable. This thought leads me again to murder, to domestic murders and gang killings and... what? If I look back at the police investigations I have played a part in over the past twelve years – murders and attempted murders – I can see only two motives overall. One was revenge and the other was the need to silence someone. These are motives I can understand. People do kill out of greed, I know, though I find that harder to believe in as a motive. Revenge I understand though, and I can imagine being backed into a corner, where everything I cared about was going to be taken away from me and the only way to survive was to silence the person who was threatening to blow my life to pieces. So what had Rebecca Clarke done? What injury could she have committed to bring down such vengeance? Or what did she know? What secret did she hold so dangerous that it had to be throttled out of her? Somebody on that video knows the answer.

So I watch it again, and this time I give it my full attention all the way through, from the childhood videos onwards, and I intend to go right through to weep my way through the girls singing at the end, except that I am arrested before I get there by an expression on a face. That wife. I misread her the first couple of times but now I think I read that look aright. It is an appeal. It says, *Will somebody please understand what is going on here?* I rerun the sequence and freeze the moment. Am I reading too much into this? I don't think so. Greed after all, then, of a sort. Lust. What everyone assumed, I suppose, from the start.

David sounds weary when he answers his phone, but perhaps it's just the prospect of talking to me that dampens his spirits. I tell him what I think I have seen.

'Watch the video again yourself,' I say. 'Look at her face. And look at him. There's a story there. And it makes sense with the phone business, doesn't it?'

'And the motive?'

'It's the usual wretched motive, isn't it? He wants her and can't have her, but he's a man who feels entitled to have what he wants, so he rapes her and then disposes of her.'

I hear him draw a breath as though he is about to say something, but then he seems to change his mind.

'Actually, that's where I started from with this – the idea of women being disposable. Amy Robsart took me there,' I say.

'It's just your story, Gina. We can't poss—'

'Have you got any other leads? It's all gone very quiet as far as I can see. Have you actually got any leads?'

'There's a lot of routine work going on. That's how these cases get cleared up in the end. You may find that uninspiring but—'

'OK, then do a routine search. Search his house. The boy's phone has to be somewhere. And I've been kept in ignorance, of course, but what about a weapon?'

'We have the weapon, the phone may well have been thrown away and I can't apply for a search warrant on the grounds that someone I know thinks the wife had a funny look on her face.'

As I am registering my demotion on the scale of *lover, partner, girlfriend* or *significant other* to *someone I know*, he rings off.

'Search the school, David,' I snarl into my dead phone. 'This thing begins and ends there. Search the damned school, why don't you?'

Chapter Twenty-Two

CIRCUIT BREAKER

May 11th

'Bingo!' Tom Ireland said as he put his head round his superintendent's door.

'Something?' Scott asked, pushing his chair back from his desk. 'Not the phone?'

'No. Not that good, I'm afraid, but photos.'

Scott was conscious of a mild churn of nausea.

'Explicit?' he asked.

'Not exactly.' Tom Ireland came further into the room and closed the door behind him. Then he handed Scott an evidence bag.

The two photos had been placed in the transparent bag back to back so Scott could see both without opening the bag. Rebecca Clarke smiled out at him, guilelessly semi-naked in a sequined bra top and a tiny matching skirt. She was heavily made up, her hair was piled on the top of her head with feathers in it, and she stood with one hand on a jutting hip – a sixteen-year-old posing as a vamp.

'School play. They did *Guys and Dolls* last year,' Tom Ireland said, 'and she was one of the Hot Box dancers.'

'How do you know that?'

'He told me.'

'He was there?'

'Came with the keys to let us in.'

'And where did you find these?'

'In his office. In a desk drawer.'

'Any other photos there?'

'Nope. Only these, and a Christmas card – from Rebecca.'

He handed over a second evidence bag containing a conventional virgin and child card.

'I won't handle it,' Scott said. 'What was the message?'

'With thanks for all your support this year, from Rebecca (Clarke).'

'Is it normal for pupils to send Christmas cards like that?'

'He says a number do.'

'But this is the only one he kept.'

'Apparently.'

'How does he explain that?'

'End of term, busy time, he must just have slipped it into the drawer without thinking. It's easier to lie when your interrogator has to keep two metres away from you.'

'And he left it there without opening the drawer again?'

'I don't think so.'

'No. But thinking isn't good enough, is it? What sort of alibi does he have for the morning she was killed? You checked staff alibis, presumably?'

'Yes. He claimed he was having breakfast with his children. He's all into discipline and routine during lockdown, apparently. He and the children are up by seven thirty every morning as if it's a normal school day.'

'Just the kind of alibi we don't want. If he's making them lie for him, nobody wants the job of trying to break them down. What about his wife?'

'She was in bed. He gets the kids up and out for fitness exercise in the garden before Zoom classes, and she gets up later.'

And if Gina is right, Scott thought, *that will get her out of lying for her husband.*

156

'It's something, Tom,' he said, 'but it's not much. It's a long way from keeping a photo and a Christmas card to murder, isn't it?'

'Yup. But these aren't normal times. People are cracking up. There was something about him today – all wound up.'

'As he might be, having his office searched.'

'More than that. On the edge, I would say.'

'So what's your scenario exactly?'

'He's obsessed with Rebecca. Maybe at school he finds reasons to get her alone – that *all your support* in her card must mean something. Now he can't see her and the obsession builds until the only thing to do is to get rid of her. I wouldn't be surprised if he had been stalking her before these breakfasts with the kids. Maybe he tried something on and she showed she was disgusted.'

'But no sexual assault.'

'It's a pretty exposed place down by the river there, even early in the morning. And then there's DNA. He would know that he could be tested.'

'Sounds pretty cold-blooded.'

'Well, it was. Getting hold of Josh's phone, writing the fake texts, getting a cover for Rebecca's phone so we would be sure to get the texts, carrying the electric flex until he got to Josh's house. It was all planned.'

'Where are you going with it now?'

'Interview him formally – put the pressure on. Talk to the children and the wife. See if any of them were aware of him going out in the early mornings. Then, if we get anything to justify it, get a warrant and search the house, shed, garage – see if there's any more of that flex. Or Josh's phone, of course, if it's not in the river.'

'If he's the killer you think he is, he'll have kept it. He's a man who likes to be in control. Throwing something away makes it unpredictable.'

157

'Let's hope.' Tom Ireland stopped at the door on his way out. 'Good idea of yours searching the offices, boss. We searched the kids' lockers but... well, it was those text messages that made us think we were looking for one of the kids.'

'As they were intended to. You'll use Teams for the interviews?'

'Yes. I'd like to get him in a small room and get in his face but...'

'How old are the kids?'

'Thirteen and fifteen.'

'Obviously they don't have to have a parent with them for a witness interview, but if their mother wants to be there, you'll let her?'

'Yes. And we'll make sure that Dad isn't hovering in earshot. An urgent need to have him down at the school while a couple of uniforms search the lockers again, I think.'

'Good. And I'd like to be an observer on those calls, Tom.'

'Okey dokey.'

And if Tom Ireland was offended by the idea of being monitored, he gave no sign of it.

Chapter Twenty-Three

ESSENTIAL TRAVEL

May 12ᵗʰ

She was going home. Flights were starting to Italy, so Nonna and Nonno were going home, and Mum had rung, all brisk and businesslike and *I'm not listening to any argument*. Freda didn't really want to argue, but she wasn't going to let Mum know that, and she did think it was way over the top for Mum to have contacted the police to get permission for her to travel home. Really? But there was this story going around about Boris's special adviser travelling with COVID, so perhaps everyone was getting twitchy.

Gary was going to drive her home in his taxi – Granny had arranged it – and Mum wanted her home in time to spend a couple of days with Nonna and Nonno before they went home, just so they didn't think she was avoiding them, though she was really. So she only had a couple of days to finish things off here, and it felt very odd because this had become normal life.

The main thing she needed to do was her sketch of the square with the trees in blossom, and she was combining this with saying goodbye to the girls. They had their routine now – walking the dogs and then settling for a chat on the benches in the square, so Granny had made a goodbye chocolate cake and they were going to eat that this morning, with a flask of lemon and ginger tea. Then the girls would go home, except for Ruby, who was going to stay and keep her company while she sketched and Granny took Flossie back home. It was a concession on Granny's part, leaving her alone, and she bet it wouldn't be long before she came back to check on her.

She was a bit worried about Granny, actually. She seemed to be at a loose end, and wound up and twitchy. She had stopped coming up with ideas for things to do or to watch on TV and she was spending a lot of time in her room or knitting that blessed blanket. She had talked about going back with Freda and having Gary drop her off at her flat in London, but Eve had been really upset and said that Granny was going back on their deal, so Granny said she would stay until she had finished the blanket. It was like the story of Penelope in reverse, Freda thought. Granny was knitting furiously so that she could be released and go home, whereas Penelope wove her tapestry all day but unravelled it every night because she had promised to marry one of her suitors when it was finished. The suitors were horrible, of course – greedy and drunk and aggressive. When she was younger, she had thought that Penelope should just have sent them all away – she was the queen, after all – but now she understood much better just how frightening men could be. Not Ben, who didn't seem to mind being bossed about by Mum, but Grandpa was definitely scary, and Lavender had to tiptoe round him. And then there was Paul. He was still in his house; Freda could see him sometimes from her bedroom window, mooching about his garden, smoking. Eve had heard from Elise that she had gone into a women's refuge after she came out of hospital, because Paul was still in the house and the police hadn't decided yet whether to charge him with assault or whatever – and anyway, they said he wouldn't be remanded in prison even if he was charged. So he was free and she was locked up. It wasn't fair and she thought it was one of the things that was making Granny miserable.

She would be quite glad to be home, where there were fewer people to worry about.

Chapter Twenty-Four

OPENING UP

May 14ᵗʰ

Freda has gone. I must try not to be too dramatic about this. She has gone back to her family, and though I think she has enjoyed herself here and I can't believe that she would have been able to write her excellent History project without a room of her own to work in, she wanted to go. She hid it well, of course, and even wept a bit as she hugged Eve goodbye, but she was grinning her head off as she waved goodbye from the back of Gary's lovely car. (Gary, by the way, was over the moon about this long-distance commission . *You're a life-saver, Gina,* he said when I rang him, and I didn't remind him that last year he had literally helped to save my life. It would have embarrassed him.)

So now here I am, and the dynamic in the house has changed. Now I am a spare part in Eve's and Colin's marriage and I don't feel comfortable. I could have gone with Freda and Gary, and Freda would have enjoyed a drive through empty London streets. In the unlikely event of our being stopped and asked our reason for travelling, I could have claimed to be escorting Freda, whose travel has been given police approval. But Eve became quite fierce about my staying; finishing the blanket has become the price of my release. I am staying because Eve wants me to and I can't resist being needed, but the requirement to finish the blanket makes me feel like a character from a myth or a fairy tale. I can't put my finger on who exactly. In the Greek myths it is always men who have tasks imposed on them, so fairy tale, I think, and I am a bit hazy about the more obscure ones. Rumpelstiltskin? Doesn't a girl have to complete a task before morning? I don't think that's it, though. Perhaps I'm inventing this.

The blanket thing niggles away at me more than it should, and so does something that hovers on the edge of my mind about Italy. Ben's parents are returning to Italy because, although people are not generally being allowed to fly around, Italians are now being allowed to go home. I didn't quite believe it so I checked it out, and it is true that people with 'essential business' in Italy (and that includes living there, I assume) are allowed, and this is somehow disturbing me.

The third thing that is getting to me is the silence from David. Has he done anything at all as a result of my phone call, or has he simply filed it under *Gina's intuition – ignore*? I am pondering all this as I sit in my usual spot in Eve's living room, knitting my umpteenth yellow square and half listening to *From Our Own Correspondent*, when light dawns. *Italy.*

Chapter Twenty-Five

VIRTUAL REALITY

May 14th

Tom Ireland had made a good choice in bringing in DC Rula Bartosz to help with interviewing the kids. And it turned out that it was a good decision to interview them both together. Scott had been against it – normal practice was to interview separately and pick up discrepancies – but the interaction of these two was quite revealing. The fifteen-year-old boy, Mark, was suspicious, bordering on aggressive, but Mira, his younger sister, was more flexible; she responded to Rula's gentle questioning and thought about her answers. She looked to her brother sometimes, when a new question came up, as if for guidance, but Scott never saw him look at her. *Is that just because she is younger, or is this a family where males are deferred to?* he wondered. He would quite have liked Gina to see this. Opinionated and impatient though she was, and with zero respect for police methods, she was also a good reader of people and, as she claimed, something of an expert on teenagers. The mother was visible in the children's Teams box, hovering in the background, occasionally looking as though she wanted to intervene but thinking better of it, Scott noticed.

Rula Bartosz was taking a good line with them, giving no hint that anyone was a suspect.

'To tell you the truth,' she said, 'we're very short of information from the public in this investigation. Usually with a murder case – especially of a young person like Rebecca – our phones are red-hot with people wanting to tell us about things they saw or heard. A lot of it isn't helpful – it's not relevant or people have even made things up – but we sift through it all and find the nuggets that will help us. This time, though, we've had hardly anything. We have been in lockdown, of course, so fewer people have been around, and Rebecca was killed quite early in the morning, but she was in a public space and some people still go jogging or cycling early in the morning, don't they? So we're thinking they may have seen something and not realised that it was relevant. That's why we're asking these questions.'

'Why are you asking us particularly?' Mark asked.

Rula smiled. 'We happen to know that you're an early morning family. Breakfast at seven thirty even during lockdown, isn't that right?'

Mira smiled back. 'On the dot,' she said.

'And do you ever go out for a run before breakfast?'

'Absolutely not,' Mark said. 'Can't help you.'

'But your dad is quite a fitness guy, isn't he? Does he ever go out jogging or cycling before breakfast?'

'Why don't you ask him?' Mark challenged.

'Oh, we will,' Rula said smoothly. 'We've chatted a lot with your dad about things at school, but we haven't got round to home yet. We'll be having a chat with him soon, though.'

Mira said, 'Dad does sometimes cycle in the early morning, in normal times, but I don't know about now. He always has his shorts on at breakfast, ready for the *get fit* stuff we do afterwards, so it's hard to tell if he's been out. He is a bit sweaty sometimes, though.' She paused and frowned. 'Actually, that was at the beginning. I think he's slacked off a bit now.'

'You don't think he goes out in the morning anymore?'

Mira glanced at her brother. 'I don't think so,' she said.

'I don't expect you remember if he was sweaty the day Rebecca was killed?'

Mark broke in impatiently. 'How would she remember? We didn't know that day was going to turn out to be different from all the others, did we?'

'Good point.' Rula smiled at him. 'And actually, we are interested in the other days as well – particularly before Rebecca's death – because we think it is quite likely that whoever killed Rebecca stalked her beforehand and found out where she went running in the mornings and at what time, so anyone who went along there in the days before her death might have noticed someone acting suspiciously. So it would be helpful to know when your dad went out.'

Mark shrugged. 'You'll have to ask him,' he said.

'We certainly will. Thank you both for your help. We'll just have a quick word with your mum and then – oh, just one thing. Did you know Rebecca?'

'We saw her around at school,' Mira said. 'We thought she was really cool, me and my friends.'

'Did you think she was cool, Mark?' Rula asked.

'Not particularly.'

'Well, thank you both,' she said. 'I'll let you go.'

The two of them moved off the screen and Tom Ireland spoke for the first time, taking charge of the interview with their mother. 'Bright kids,' he said. 'You and your husband must be proud of them.'

'Aren't parents always proud of their children?' she said, sitting down in one of the vacated seats. She was close to the camera now and though she was carefully made up, her face looked crumpled and not healthy. The fitness and exercise regime didn't extend to her, Scott thought.

'You're probably right,' Tom Ireland said affably. 'You seem like a close family, anyway. Are you?'

166

'We have our moments.' Her tone was guarded and her eyes were watchful.

'But you don't care for early mornings?'

'I can get up early when I have to but sleeping in has been a bonus while we're locked down.'

'So it must be annoying to be disturbed by your husband getting up for early morning cycle rides.'

'If he does go out, he doesn't disturb me.'

'Really? You do share a room, do you?'

'We certainly do.'

There was an emphasis there, Scott noticed – an inflection that said *and we have sex*.

'But what your husband does in the early morning is a mystery to you – and what the children are doing, I suppose?'

'My husband has them organised, as you heard.'

'And do you take part in the *keep fit* exercise after breakfast?'

'No. I have my own online pilates class later in the day.'

'A bit less strenuous?'

'It keeps me trim. My husband is a very energetic man.'

Again, Scott thought, there was that implication that she was talking about sex. But she hadn't finished.

'Actually, pilates is rather too tame for me. I normally do a weekly karate class – but that's something you can't do online.'

'That's unusual – karate,' he said.

'More women should do it. We need to be able to protect ourselves. I shall start Mira on classes soon.'

'Well,' Tom Ireland said, 'thank you. It's a pity that you can't help to jog your husband's memory about his early morning outings, but we'll see if his memory has got any clearer when he gets back from the school.'

'I can go?'

'Yes.'

And there was that look again, the one Gina had noticed from the video. An odd look that you could read either as challenge or as appeal.

She is the one who might break, Scott thought. *The boy may suspect, but the wife's the one who could break if we can keep the pressure on.*

The husband wasn't looking like breaking. Questioned on his return from the locker search at the school, he smoothly acknowledged the occasional morning cycle ride early on in lockdown – *Good intentions. Not so good now, I'm afraid* – but claimed that his regular route took him nowhere near the river – *Path gets too narrow and you can't keep the speed up.* Pressed again about the photo and card in his desk drawer, he gave the same answer – *Lovely girl, very like her to send a card.* The photo? Suggestive? *Oh really, what could be more innocent than that photo? A thoroughly nice girl playing at being sexy.*

Tom Ireland got nowhere with him; Scott wondered whether Rula might have done better. As he sat turning over possible lines of attack (could they find grounds to search the house?) his phone rang and the caller ID made his heart sink. Gina. He let it ring out. She would keep ringing and he would have to answer eventually, but he needed to shore up his defences first.

Ten minutes later, fortified with a cup of coffee, he answered her at her third time of calling.

'Italy, David,' she said. 'It's been bugging me and now I've got it. Freda's gone home, you see.'

'Gina, I have no idea what you are talking about.'

'That's because you haven't been keeping me in the loop. I've been sitting here for days with my knitting, waiting for you to tell me you've followed up on our conversation, and the one thing that has comforted me in the face of the tortoise-like pace of your investigation – I would say *glacial* but the glaciers are moving fast these days – the one thing that has comforted me is that he can't go anywhere. If he panics, if you are putting any pressure on – and I don't know that you are – he's stuck here, because nobody can go anywhere. Except that they can. Freda is going home because there will be room for her at home because Ben's parents are returning to Italy. Italy, David, to which exiles are allowed to return, along with anyone else who has urgent business there.'

'You keep saying *Italy* as though that should mean something.'

'His name. Look at his name. And his looks, if it comes to that. No Englishman has that kind of good looks. I bet you he has family in Italy and can make a case for an urgent need to visit. And half term is coming up. If he goes then, no-one but his family will know until he's not back on Zoom classes a week later.'

She was speaking very fast. Scott took in a deep breath and made a bid to slow the pace.

'Let's think about this for a moment, shall we? Let's suppose that he could and did get himself to Italy. We'd have no problem getting him sent back if we said we needed him for questioning, and he must know that.'

'Really? I have a colleague who has a holiday place in Italy, and he says the whole place runs on bribes. You can fix anything if you know who to pay.'

'That may apply to getting your water supply laid on, but not to the police.'

'Absolutely to the police. Rife with corruption.'

'Well, I doubt it and I think you're working from Italian films that you watched in your impressionable youth, but thank you for the heads-up. We'll bear it in mind.'

'I wish we were having this conversation in person.'

'Why?'

'So I could slap your patronising face.'

Scott allowed a pause.

169

'Is there anything else I can do for you, Ms Gray?' he asked.

'Yes. Tell me what's going on. Have you done a search? What have you found? Have you questioned him? What about DNA?'

'You know quite well that I can't tell you any of that, but I will tell you – though why, I don't know – that we are pursuing that line of inquiry, along with a number of others.'

'And here endeth the press statement.'

'No. Strictly for your ears only.'

He clicked off his phone.

Half an hour later, he roused himself from thought and rang Tom Ireland.

'We haven't had to think about flight risk, Tom,' he said, 'for obvious reasons, but the only way we're going to get this guy is if he or one of the family breaks, so we're going to have to keep the pressure on, and if we do that he might just panic and try to do a runner. Limited flights are starting up again, aren't they? So—'

'Monitor any bookings in the name of Murano? Shouldn't be difficult with the small numbers.'

'Good. It might actually be how we get him – if we can push him hard enough.'

'We're on it.'

Chapter Twenty-Six

EXIT STRATEGY

May 23ʳᵈ

Well, who'd have thought it? David has actually listened to me, it seems, and had the decency to let me know that they are on the look-out for signs that Philip Murano is about to go on the run. He told me this a week ago, and since then I have been on the proverbial tenterhooks. (Do you know what those are, by the way? Or *were*, rather. They were the nails round the edge of a wooden frame (a *tenter*) on which woollen cloth was stretched back in the grubby old days when wool was woven straight from the sheep, grease, muck and all, and then washed and stretched out to dry – under tension. Weaving is all over the place in our vocabulary, actually – *shoddy*, meaning rubbishy cloth made from discarded wool, or *warp*, the lengthwise threads that were thrown onto a loom, or *fast* for dyes that are fixed.) But I am skidding off my narrative path. The point is that David and his team are on the case of Philip Murano, deputy head of Greenacres High School. His video tribute to Rebecca gave him away. It was too much – the poem, the emotion, and finally the tears. They went well beyond the conventional tribute of a teacher to a pupil, however tragic the circumstances. He was in thrall to her, I suppose, and killed her because she couldn't and wouldn't be his. Was his collapse at the end of his tribute actually the realisation of what he had done? And his wife knew, of course. That was what that moment meant, when she came into view behind him and looked directly into the camera. *Will somebody see this and help me?*

David's team need evidence, of course, and Murano has been clever, so all they can do is keep the pressure on him until he panics. And I hesitate to tell you this, but I have actually put some pressure on him myself. It is surprisingly easy to get hold of a telephone number, via a modest subscription to a website. I am not going to say more about what I have done because I think David would never speak to me again if he knew and I am afraid now that I may have made a mistake. The intention was to get him to panic and go on the run, but there is more than one way of panicking. What haunts me now, and has done in the days since I made my phone call, is the fear that he might go for the nuclear option and kill himself – and his family. Because that's what men will do when things run out of their control, isn't it?

So I am in a state where I both long for and dread a phone call from David and approach each news broadcast with sweaty trepidation. This has been going on for days, but today is crisis point. It's the first day of the half term break, the day I have always imagined as the time he will choose to make his move. He will think he can trust his wife to keep quiet, and that will give him a week and two weekends before the school starts to wonder where he is. Does he have family in Italy? Cousins? The name makes me think of Venice but they could be anywhere, I suppose – in a city where he can get lost in the throng, or in a village that the forces of the law mainly leave alone. David may be right in suggesting that my picture of Italy is skewed, derived entirely from old films, crime novels and occasional tourist forays, but if I am right, then I ought to get news soon, always supposing that David thinks to let me know. Actually, if he has made an arrest, he won't need to ring me. It will be news.

By mid-afternoon I am so reconciled to hearing nothing that when my phone rings it makes me jump. It is David.

'Well?' I say.

'Well, you were wrong.'

'You don't know that. It's early days. He might try in a day or two.'

'We've made an arrest.'

'You've arrested him already? Well then, I wasn't wr—'

'We've arrested someone else.'

'Not that poor boy? Oh David, he didn't—'

'Not Josh Clements, no. A fully paid-up adult.'

'So who?'

'We made the arrest at Gatwick airport this morning, so you were right about that.'

I am bewildered. 'Not that crabby headmaster?' I ask. 'But he's not—'

'Italian. No. Full credit to you for that. We put out a check on flights booked in the name of Murano just as you suggested, and bingo.'

I realise for the first time in this conversation that he is in a state of high excitement, quite uncharacteristic of him. He's like an actor coming off stage after a good performance.

'Tell me,' I say. 'Were you actually there?'

'I was. Poor old Tom Ireland is self-isolating. His wife's a nurse and she's gone down with COVID symptoms. They're waiting for the results of her test.'

'So you actually wielded the handcuffs?'

'I wasn't alone. But it isn't easy to be inconspicuous in an almost empty departures area. I had a DS and a DC trying to look like a honeymooning couple, and I hung around scanning the board. We had bags with us to make us credible as travellers, but I was afraid they were just going to alert security to our odd behaviour. It began to look as though she wasn't going to show, though she had made the booking. She didn't arrive until the last minute.'

'She?' My voice comes out in an inelegant squeak.

'Lucy Murano.'

'His wife?'

'His wife – and the headmaster's secretary. That's what we failed to take account of, and I am ashamed about that.'

'But not ashamed of failing to pass that very useful piece of information to me? How was I supposed to—'

'You weren't supposed to do anything, Gina. The last time I looked—'

'Oh for God's sake! Cliché alert. *The last time I looked you weren't an employee of the Metropolitan Police.* I am useful to you, admit it.'

'I do. And it wasn't confidential information that Lucy Murano worked at the school. We just didn't see the significance. We had her in two separate boxes. We should have seen that she, more than anyone, had access to Josh's phone, but her husband wasn't a suspect at that point.'

'Until I pointed you that way.'

'But you were wrong about the look on her face on the video.'

'Not completely. I saw that it was an appeal for help.'

'But for herself, for what she'd done? Maybe.'

'Are you going to tell me what she's said?'

'Nothing at the moment.'

'Oh, come on…'

'Truthfully. She was all outraged dignity when we arrested her. You would have liked her outfit by the way – very svelte and Italian. Claimed that she was going to Veneto on her husband's behalf to deal with his grandmother's estate – she having died of COVID. We're checking that, of course, but in the meantime she is saying nothing.'

'So that could be true, couldn't it? Do you actually have any evidence against her? Or a motive? Just jealousy? Of a teenager? It sounds pretty feeble.'

'We're searching the house. Her husband is cooperating. He knew, I think.'

'You're sure it wasn't him? You still might have the wrong—'

'I've thought all along that the killer might be female.'

'Why? It's so unusual, isn't it – for that sort of killing?'

'At its crudest, no sexual interference. With the murder of a girl, that's extremely unusual. And I thought Rebecca would have been off her guard with a woman or girl.'

'I assumed that she had been raped. You kept that out of the news. And strangling? Do women strangle other women?'

'Lucy Murano does karate.'

'That doesn't involve strangling, does it?'

'No, but it's unarmed combat. You learn where the weak points are.'

'I'm still not sure I believe it.'

'That's because you think that aggressors are always men and victims always women.'

'Of course I don't'

'Except verbally, of course. In your code, women are allowed any amount of verbal coshing.'

'If she did do it, what do you think her motive was?'

'I don't know. She has a lot of pride and she's married to a man who is good-looking and knows it. I imagine a lot of the girls have crushes on him, but Rebecca seems to have got under his skin. Lockdown is doing odd things to people. Maybe she became obsessive about her. We won't know unless she talks.'

'Those poor children.'

'Rebecca, her sister, Josh Clements, Mark and Mira Murano. This thing's taken a terrible toll on the young.'

'Will you tell me what she says?'

There is a pause.

'Probably not,' he says.

Chapter Twenty-Seven

UNMUTE

May 23rd

The Murano house was on what would no doubt have been advertised as an executive estate, although the houses didn't quite live up to that description. Detached they were but only just, the gaps between them being so narrow they might as well have been terraced really. As Scott drew up behind the police van outside the house, he noticed that two cars were parked in the drive. Of course Lucy Murano would not have taken her own car to the airport – she taxied, no doubt, leaving her smart little Fiat in the drive as deflection. Scott got out of his car and surveyed the front of the house. The developers had aimed at vaguely nineteenth century elegance with pillars and carriage lamps flanking the front door; but the pillars, he thought, were too skinny and the carriage lamps too flimsy to be convincing. Realising that he was in danger of making the place a metaphor for the Murano family itself, he walked briskly up the drive and almost collided with a uniformed officer who was struggling backwards out of the front door, carrying a desktop computer. He attempted an acknowledgement of Scott's rank as he passed him to load the computer into the van.

Inside the house there was an atmosphere of quiet concentration. This was not the kind of frantic search that they sometimes show in TV dramas. A team of four officers was quietly and methodically going from room to room. Objects were being removed and slipped carefully into evidence bags, there was the occasional murmured exchange, and from upstairs came the sounds of doors and drawers being opened and closed.

Scott stood in the hall and took in the scene. Through an open door he could see Philip Murano sitting on a sofa, his head in his hands, and beyond, through the plate glass window behind him, he could see the children in the garden, playing a listless game of badminton. Murano appeared not to hear him as he went into the room, so he touched him gently on the shoulder before stepping back to maintain distance between them. The man started and looked up at Scott with bloodshot eyes. He was almost unrecognisable as the sleek, charismatic character who had delivered that moving eulogy on the Clarke family's tribute video. Scott had seen people in despair before – guilty, trapped, terrified – but he thought he had never seen someone so completely altered, not just as though he had peeled off a remarkably lifelike mask, but as though the life itself had been in the mask.

'What have you told the children?' he asked quietly.

Murano looked over his shoulder into the garden. 'Nothing as yet,' he said. He attempted a smile and the result was grotesque. 'I took a leaf out of your book. *Routine enquiries*, I told them.'

One of the search team came into the room and hesitated just inside the door. He was holding an evidence bag and Scott could see from across the room that what it contained was a mobile phone. He walked across to him and steered him back into the hall.

'Her phone?' he asked quietly.

'Out of charge, sir, but I don't think so. He,' he nodded in the direction of the sitting room, 'took us to it. Under the wife's *lingerie*.' He pronounced the word with a leer. 'And very fancy stuff it is too,' he said, the grin on his face fading as Scott looked stonily back at him. 'Could be the boy's,' he mumbled. 'Josh Clements's. That's what he thinks.' Again he nodded in the direction of Philip Murano.

Scott put out a hand for the phone. 'I'm heading back to the station,' he said. 'I'll get it straight to Forensics and we'll see what's on it.'

Going back into the sitting room, he dangled the evidence in front of Murano. 'How did you know where this was?' he asked.

Murano muttered something he couldn't catch.

'What did you say?'

Murano looked up. 'She hid things there,' he said. 'Things she didn't want the children to find. Birthday presents...' he tailed off and half turned his head to gaze vaguely out into the garden.

'You knew she had Josh's phone.'

'I guessed.'

'Because you knew she had killed Rebecca?'

Murano flinched as though he had been slapped, but he said nothing.

'Did she tell you she had done it?'

'No.' He put his head back in his hands.

'Did she know that you had guessed?'

Murano shook his head but didn't look up. 'I don't know,' he said.

'And what made you think that she had done it, Mr Murano?'

Now Murano did look up and his mouth opened into what seemed at first to be a wide smile. Then he started to sob. He was saying something through the sobs that Scott couldn't decipher at first. Then he heard it.

'It was my fault,' he was saying. 'It was all my fault. I'm the killer.'

Scott left him to pull himself together and went upstairs. The officers up there barely acknowledged him, intent on their search. Scott remembered that state during a search – that intense concentration, methodical and hyper-alert, that put you into a kind of trance. He went into a small room that was obviously used as an office. The desk under the window was almost bare but presumably had housed the computer that he had seen being carried out. Philip Murano's? He wondered if Lucy Murano had a computer of her own. She sat at a computer most of the time at work, he imagined; perhaps she didn't use one at home. Or did she use her husband's? And what would be on a computer that was relevant to this murder anyway? Emails, possibly?

He broke the silence. 'Anything?' he asked.

The DC who was going through the desk drawers looked round and pointed to a crate containing some files and other apparently random objects. 'In there, sir,' she said. 'More photos and stuff. In the flat box.'

Scott slipped on gloves and lifted the small box out. It had originally contained an expensive pen set, he could see; a presentation gift box with a fountain pen and matching ballpoint, he guessed – unnecessarily large for its contents, which would have nestled in satiny beds. Now, he saw as he lifted the lid off, it held a small archive dedicated to Rebecca Clarke. Some more photos: one in DofE trekking gear, grinning cheerfully; one pensive, snapped without her being aware, he thought; and one accepting a trophy for the athletics team. Under those was a card from Rebecca – a flowery card with a message of thanks: *Dear Mr Murano, thank you so much for all your extra help with my English this term. I feel much more confident about the course now. Rebecca x.* Did she wonder about putting that 'x'? Or was it what they all used to everyone on cards, emails, texts? Did he read it as encouragement, attached as it was to a very standard note of thanks from student to teacher?

He looked again at the photos. *Guileless* was the word that came to mind when you looked at that open smile. Had she any idea of the feelings she stirred in him? The card was undated. Had Murano become more pressing once the lockdown was in place and he had no excuse for seeing her for *extra help*? Had he become more obvious, stalking her in the early mornings? Rebecca's mother had said that she was thinking of stopping the morning runs and going out at another time. Was she trying to avoid him? If so, why was Lucy Murano's jealousy so powerful that it drove her to murder?

He wasn't going to get close to knowing until he got Lucy Murano to talk – and for that he needed evidence that would shake her. He felt for the phone in its bag in his pocket and headed back downstairs.

At the station, he went straight to the lab to hand over the phone. 'Top priority,' he said. 'Let me know if it belongs to Joshua Clements, and check the text messages. Anything of interest from the house so far?'

'We're just getting into the PC,' came the answer. 'Moving as fast as we can.' The tone was a practised one – *Such prima donnas, these senior officers*, it said. *Just trust the professionals to do their job.*

As he was walking to his office, his phone rang and he looked at the caller ID, making a bet with himself that it would be either Gina or Tom Ireland, both desperate for updates. He was grateful to find that it was Tom, who wouldn't try to tell him how to handle his interview with Lucy Murano.

'Tom. How's Debbie?'

'Not bad. Fed up, though. Still no results from her test.'

'I'm really sorry you can't be here for the kill, Tom, when you've worked so hard on this case.'

'Just make sure you nail her, that's all I ask.'

'We will. We think we've got Josh Clements's phone, retrieved from her underwear drawer, would you believe?'

'You *think* you've got it?'

'It's out of charge. I'm waiting to hear from the lab.'

'Her underwear drawer? Jesus. That's kinky, isn't it?'

'It's where she habitually hides things, apparently. Her husband led us to it.'

'He knew?'

'He had a pretty good idea.'

'You haven't interviewed her yet?'

'I'd like some hard evidence to present her with – the phone, ideally. She'll have a story worked out and I'll need to shake her.'

'You're giving her more time to polish the story, though.'

'All to the good, I think. She's likely to over-egg it.'

'You're the boss.'

'I'll let you know as soon as there's news.'

At his desk, he looked at the information that Rula Bartosz had left about Lucy Murano. It was, in fact, taken from the filing cabinet in Lucy's own office, where staff CVs were kept. Scott glanced through it and found that, of course, it offered no hint of a clue that this was a woman who might kill in cold blood. Born Lucy Jane Harrison in Felixstowe in 1979, she had attended a local state school and then took a degree in business and finance at Oxford Brookes University, graduating with a 2:1 in 2000. In that year she also married Philip Rafaele Murano. She had worked as a PA in a city law firm for five years before the birth of her first child in 2005, followed by a second child in 2008. In 2012 she had started her job at Greenacres High School. She listed her interests as reading, film, modern dance and karate.

It was remarkably bland. The karate, Scott supposed, might mark her out – and perhaps the modern dance. The CV dated back to 2012, of course. She was still doing the karate, they knew, but if she was still dancing, what would that be about? Idly, he drew circles round *karate* and *dance*. She must be pretty good at the karate by now, he thought, and that in itself would be a good reason for carrying on with it – a boost to self-esteem for a woman of forty with two adolescent children and a humdrum job. But what had triggered the interest in karate to start with? Aggression that needed channelling, or fear? Had Lucy Murano ever been attacked? The search he had ordered on her had produced no police record of any kind, apart from one speeding ticket. If she had ever suffered a serious assault, it had not been reported. Aggression, then? He moved his pen across to *dance* and thickened the circle round it. Had she danced since childhood? Did she dream once of being a dancer? In 2012, with two small children, was this her weekly hour of glamour? She could have gone for ballroom dancing, couldn't she, and taken her husband with her? They would certainly have made a glamorous couple. But she didn't – the dancing was hers alone, and she carried it with her. He had watched her that morning, walking into the departures area, tall, blonde, groomed – overdressed, really, for a plane journey, in a cream silk coat and killer heels, but turning heads and knowing it.

So which was it? Fear? Aggression? Vanity? Which of those would press her buttons? Which was going to unmute her?

When he looked in through the window to the interview room she was still looking composed, sitting behind a COVID-safe Perspex screen, which gave the incongruous impression that she was in an oversized Zoom box. She had taken off the cream coat and draped it over the back of her chair. Underneath she was wearing a matching cream skirt and a caramel silk shirt. She was still wearing the spiky heels, and as he and Rula Bartosz entered the room, he wondered briefly whether the custody sergeant had thought of removing them as potential weapons.

She stood up as they came in, and picked up her coat. 'Good,' she said. 'I hope this means that this muddle has been cleared up and you have come to apologise and let me go. I can't tell you how inconvenient it has been for me to miss my flight. It wasn't easy to get a flight and I have all sorts of arrangements at the other end that I need to cancel.' Her eyes slid to the phone in its evidence bag that Rula Bartosz was carrying. 'Is that my phone?' she demanded. 'Because if so, I shall be extremely glad to have it back so that I can start sorting out this morning's mess.'

You had to admire her nerve, Scott thought reluctantly. *Chutzpah*, Gina would have called it, and it went through his mind that fencing with this woman would be almost like doing battle with Gina, except he didn't need to remind himself that this woman had almost certainly murdered in cold blood a seventeen-year-old who had everything in the world to live for.

'Yes,' he said, 'the business affairs you have to see to in Italy – your husband's grandmother's estate. The grandmother who died eighteen months ago, and whose affairs have been nicely tidied up by one of her sons. Probate was granted nearly a year ago, wasn't it?'

She put her coat back onto her chair but she remained standing. 'There are still some matters that my husband is concerned about,' she said.

'But not concerned enough to go and see to them himself.'

She laughed. 'You have seen enough of the school, I'm sure, to spot that the head is something of a chocolate teapot. Philip runs the place – it couldn't function without him.'

'Not even at half term?'

'Not in the current situation.'

Her eyes slid again to the phone and he picked up his cue. 'It's a puzzle, this phone,' he said, 'because we still have your phone, you see – they're checking it out in the lab – but we also have this one, which ought to be yours, considering where it was found, but turns out not to be.'

She stared at him.

'So why don't we sit down and talk?' he said. 'And the phone is a good place to start.'

He and Rula Bartosz settled themselves on chairs the other side of her screen and some distance from her. It played to her strengths, he thought, the distancing; it made keeping cool feel like the norm. He could play the cool game too, but Rula's strength was in her warmth, her ability to make an interviewee feel her empathy. He wasn't sure that was going to happen here.

Lucy Murano took her time in arranging her coat over her chair back, and then sat down carefully. Scott leant back in his chair.

'Would you like to tell us who you think this phone belongs to?' he asked. 'Since it was found among your possessions.'

'I imagine it belongs to Joshua Clements,' she said.

'And how did it come to be among your possessions?'

'I was looking after it. He's a gormless boy. He had it confiscated and then didn't pick it up from my office the day before lockdown. I wasn't sure how easy it would be to get into the school once we were locked down, so I brought it home so he could pick it up later.'

'But your husband is the deputy headmaster. He has keys to the school.'

'I wasn't sure if it would be within the rules to use them.'

'Did you let him know that you had his phone?'

'I wasn't able to, as it happened. I was intending to call in at his mother's shop but then I realised that it would be closed.'

'So you hid it in your underwear drawer?'

'I put it there for safekeeping.'

'An odd place to put it, wasn't it?'

'I don't know if you have a family, Superintendent Scott, but there is very little privacy in a family house. I don't have an office at home, so I keep things in my bedroom.'

'Among your underwear?'

'As it happens, yes.'

She looked back at him, clear-eyed and defiant.

'And when it became common knowledge that Joshua Clements was a person of interest to us in our investigation, and that threatening text messages had been sent to Rebecca Clarke before her murder, you didn't think that it would be helpful to hand over the phone to us?'

'I don't use social media. I knew nothing about text messages.'

'They were published in a newspaper.'

'I get my news from the BBC.'

Scott stood up and walked to the window, then returned to his seat.

'Are you familiar with the *reasonable person* standard in our legal system?' he asked conversationally.

He had startled her, he could see; she wasn't sure where this was going. But she wasn't rattled yet.

'You're the expert,' she said.

'The reasonable person test gets applied quite often in court – with pleas of self-defence, for example, a jury is asked to consider what a reasonable person would be expected to do. So I ask myself what a jury would make of your story: an intelligent woman with a responsible job in a school, finding that a pupil has left his phone at school on the eve of lockdown, takes it home with her for safekeeping, despite the fact that it would be perfectly safe in the school and her husband has access to the building, should the boy want to retrieve it. Then she makes no attempt to contact the boy but stores the phone among her underwear, where she could hardly fail to be aware of it. Even so, when the boy concerned is known to be a suspect for the horrific murder of a fellow pupil and it is widely known that threatening texts were sent to the victim shortly before her death, the woman takes no action. She does not even mention the phone to the police, despite being interviewed by them. Do you think a jury would regard those as the actions of a reasonable woman?'

She uncrossed her legs and recrossed them. 'I think that the definition of *reasonable* will vary between individuals,' she said.

'But it doesn't stop there, does it?' Scott pressed. 'Perhaps you can tell me how a reasonable person could explain how two text messages were sent from that phone to Rebecca Clarke while it lay, apparently untouched, among your bras? As you say you managed to ignore the intense media interest in those messages, I am asking DC Bartosz to show you a screenshot of those messages.'

Rula Bartosz took a sheet of paper out of a folder in front of her and held it up against the Perspex screen. Lucy Murano glanced at it and then sat back in her chair.

'It's a joke, isn't it?' she said.

'A joke?' It was hard, he found, to match cool for cool. *A joke?*

'Josh Clements is a joke. They all laugh at him. He's as thick as mince – to quote the PM's special adviser – and he trailed round after that girl like a lost dog.'

'So you sent the texts as a joke, to mock him and cause trouble with Rebecca? That was remarkably cruel, wasn't it?'

She laughed. 'I didn't send them, obviously. It will have been one of my kids. Kids are cruel. I work in a school. Trust me, I know.'

'You think your children found the phone even though you had put it in your safe place?'

'Nowhere's safe in a family home. I've told you, there's no privacy.'

He allowed a pause. 'Mrs Murano,' he said, 'not much surprises me in my job anymore, but you have actually amazed me. Over the years I have been faced time and again with parents lying to me in order to protect their children. I've never before been confronted by a mother lying about her children in order to protect herself.'

She looked straight at him without a hint of shame. 'There's more than one way to protect one's children,' she said.

'And that means what? What did they need protection from? Their father's obsession with Rebecca Clarke? Didn't they know about that already?'

Her laugh this time was less convincing. 'She had a crush on him,' she said, 'like all the other silly girls. She meant no more to him than any of the others.'

'And yet it was only her photos that he kept in his desk – at home and at school.'

'Because she kept giving them to him. She behaved like a little tart.'

She closed her eyes for a moment, rerunning what she had said, and then attempted a repair. 'Of course, she was a nice girl and it was innocent, I'm sure. I didn't mean...'

'You didn't mean what, Mrs Murano?'

'That her death was anything other than a terrible tragedy.'

'Tell me about your husband's early morning cycle rides.'

'I've told you. I know nothing about them. I was sleeping in.'

'You never went out with him?'

'No.'

'Never followed him to see where he was going?'

'Of course not.'

'You do have a bike, though, don't you? We found four bikes in your garage.'

'It was an idea of my husband's a couple of years ago – family cycle rides. We do them occasionally. I don't enjoy them. I'm not what you might call an *outdoorsy* person.'

She smoothed the silky fabric of her cream skirt, making her point.

'We've taken the bikes in for forensic examination. They will look for soil traces on the tyres. It's remarkable what they can determine from seeds and plant particles – not just where the bike has been but when, in many cases.'

She leant forward. 'You're almost literally clutching at straws, Superintendent. I watch crime dramas on TV. You're desperate to get a confession out of me because you haven't got anything else. If you had any real evidence against me, you would just charge me and be done with it.'

Scott locked eyes with her, and then swung round, startled by a knock at the door. Rula Bartosz got up and went to open it. Behind her he could see Nasrin Khan from the forensic lab, waving a brown folder at him. 'Thank you, Rula,' he said, and as she returned to her place he got up and went outside to join Nasrin, who was almost bouncing with excitement.

'A screenshot from Lucy Murano's phone,' she said, thrusting a slim brown folder at him, 'and I've included a picture of Rebecca's phone so you can see.'

He opened the folder, which contained two sheets of paper. At first he was not sure what he was looking at, and then he saw that it was a screenshot of an email receipt for an online order, which helpfully included an image of the item ordered. The image was of a blue waterproof cover for a mobile phone. Turning to the second sheet, he found a photo of the cover that protected Rebecca's phone. There was no doubt that they were identical.

'And this cover was paid for from Lucy Murano's account?' he asked. 'You've checked?'

'We have.'

She stood looking expectantly at him with soulful dark eyes, a bit like a puppy expecting to be rewarded with a treat.

'Well done,' he said, and then, 'Thank you for bringing it up here. Perfect timing, Nasrin.'

She ducked her head but he saw the blush under her

honey-coloured skin before she turned and almost skipped down the corridor. He took a breath and went back into the interview room.

'Since you tell us that you're not an *outdoorsy* person, I assume that you bought this for your phone in case you wanted to use it in the shower,' he said as he sat down and held the screenshot of the receipt against the Perspex shield.

He saw the flash of panic in her eyes, but her mouth retained the slight smile that she had held in place throughout the interview.

'I bought it for Philip,' she said, 'since he is *outdoorsy*.'

'For all those early morning cycle rides that you didn't know he was doing?'

She shrugged. 'I knew he'd be out some time.'

Scott took the other sheet of paper out of the folder and displayed it next to the screenshot.

'Do you know what this is?'

'No idea.' She leant back in her chair. 'You're going to tell me, I expect.'

'It's the cover we found on Rebecca Clarke's phone when we took it from her dead body, Mrs Murano. Quite a coincidence, isn't it? Especially since you ordered an identical one just three days before she was murdered.'

'I'm afraid I don't see the connection.'

'That phone cover never belonged to Rebecca Clarke. Her fingerprints weren't on it. Fingerprints can still be found on objects that have been in water, by the way – a lot of people don't realise that. Rebecca's killer put that cover on her phone before dragging her into the river, because it was part of the plan that we should be able to read the threatening text messages sent from Joshua Clements's phone.'

She leant forward, her face almost touching the screen. 'Then you should be talking to my husband, shouldn't you?' she hissed.

'It's quite a family conspiracy you're describing for us. Your children found the phone and wrote the messages, and then your husband made use of the gift you had so thoughtfully bought for him to murder one of his pupils and deflect the blame onto another one. And you weren't aware of any of it, apparently.'

Rula Bartosz suddenly leant forward. 'Do you want to see them all in court, Mrs Murano? Your husband charged with murder and your children charged as accessories? Is that really what you want?'

Lucy Murano leant forward so that her face was almost touching the screen. 'You stupid bitch,' she said. 'Who do you think I did it for?'

Then she leant back and closed her eyes. Scott put up a hand to forestall any reaction from Rula Bartosz, and when Lucy Murano opened her eyes she looked directly at Scott.

'I got a better degree than him, you know,' she said. 'We both got 2:1s but I got better marks on the papers. And still we took it for granted that his career was going to be the important one. Why did we do that? And then he said he wanted to go into teaching and I was… devastated. We'd been the cool couple all through uni – everyone wanted to be seen with us. He could have done… anything, with his looks and charisma. And he said he wanted to be a teacher. We argued about it and in the end he persuaded me. He'd got this vision, you see – he was going to be this great, charismatic teacher, the kind that people always remember and say they changed their life. He had a plan. He would do his PGCE and then do a stint teaching in a comp in London, because that's how you earned your spurs, and then he'd get a Head of Department job somewhere nice, where we could afford a good house, and we'd settle down and have kids and be a nice little family. And he'd be a headmaster before he was forty. So that's what we did. We got married. And that was the last glamorous thing we did. We threw everything into that wedding, took out a huge loan, and it was fabulous, but then there was real life – real, dull life. He did his PGCE and I supported him. And actually, that wasn't too dull. I got a job as a PA to one of the executives in a City investment firm, and that was cool. I got the job because of my looks and my style. These execs like that – it bigs them up to have a PA who other men look at and envy. I used to get invited to join them when they were out wining and dining clients, and I was even given a clothes allowance, so that wasn't bad, and I carried on with that job while Phil did his time at the coalface in a London school. And he didn't do badly, I have to say. He worked hard and he got good results and he landed the Head of English job at Greenacres. And the result is the woman you see before you.' She suddenly held out her arms in a gesture that was somewhere between display and surrender. 'I gave up my City job, we bought the house, and it seemed that it was time to have the babies. We were very efficient – first a boy and then a girl, the obligatory two years between them. Perfect.' She looked at Rula Bartosz. 'Do you have children?' she asked.

Rula shook her head very slightly and Lucy Murano smiled. 'There's a template, you know, for doing babies, and I copied it to the millimetre. I ferried them off to swimming classes and toddler groups, I went to coffee mornings and met the other mums at Pilates classes, and it was dull, dull, dull. I swapped Pilates for Karate – a better vehicle for my aggression, you might say – but the thing that really kept me going was my dance class. I started dance when I was in London – I needed to keep fit and fight off the effects of the corporate lunches – but once I had the children, the dance classes were what kept me alive. They were my sprinkle of stardust, the glimmers of light in my grey weeks. Phil was having a whale of a time, surrounded by pretty girls who adored him. If you look at the composition of any A-level English class, you will find that it is composed of at least seventy-five per cent girls – and they love him. He kept his head – he knew what the dangers were – but we had some wobbly moments. And then, just as our daughter was starting school, the headmaster's secretary retired and there was a vacancy, and it seemed like a good idea for me to be there on the premises, where I could keep an eye on what was going on.'

She stopped speaking and sat staring into space for a moment before rubbing her hands over her face and continuing.

'Seven years I've done it for, and if you want a job where you're at everyone's beck and call, try being a school secretary. Parents have got a complaint? *Talk to my secretary, Mrs Murano.* Hit your head in the playground or come out in spots? *Go and see Mrs Murano.* Lost your mobile phone? Had your packed lunch stolen? *Report it to Mrs Murano.* I keep the EpiPens for the anaphylactics and the glucagon for the diabetics, I ferry children to A&E and I dose the Head with aspirin and Valium when it all gets too much for him. And between whiles I'm trying to keep an eye on what my bloody husband is doing. My office sits between the Head's office and his, and I never get a proper lunch break because that's when he likes to have the sweet young things in his A-level class in to go through their essays with them. I have developed the ability to eat a sandwich very, very quietly so that I can listen to what's going on next door. The school is jerry-built, of course, so the walls are paper thin, and I can hear them talking. And laughing – there's a lot of laughing because Mr Murano is super cool. It's the silences that I have to worry about, and then I've developed a whole repertoire of excuses for interrupting them. And they despise me, of course, these girls. I can highlight my hair and paint my nails and spend more than we can afford on clothes, but still I'm nobody as far as they're concerned, and nothing like good enough for our dishy and dashing Mr Murano.'

She stopped speaking suddenly and gazed into empty space.

Rula Bartosz glanced at Scott as if looking for permission, and then said very gently, 'And Rebecca Clarke? Was she different from the others?'

'Oh, she was a piece of work,' Lucy Murano said, 'with her *Oh, I'm so worried about my English, Mr Murano* and her little thank-you cards, and those photographs. She was so butter-wouldn't-melt that even I couldn't work out whether it was all calculated or whether she really was an innocent.'

'Did you talk to your husband about her?' Scott asked.

'We didn't talk about the girls. It was understood between us. We both knew what was going on. It wasn't until the lockdown came that I could see that he was obsessed with her. He couldn't see her anymore in the normal course of things and he was starting to stalk her. It was getting embarrassing; it was getting dangerous. And then I did challenge him, and he promised it was going to stop and it would all be fine, but it wasn't going to stop and it wouldn't be fine. He was out there on his bike, following her when she was out for runs. He was mooning about the place, and I couldn't see how it could end well. If she gave in to him it would end in a scandal, and if she didn't, she would end up making a complaint about him, and there would still be a scandal. Either way it was the end of his career – it was the end of our lives. I had to find a way out of it. It was down to me.'

'And you decided that killing her was the answer?'

'I couldn't see any other way out. What would you have done?'

'Taking Joshua Clements' phone,' Scott said, 'that looks like planning ahead.'

'That was fortuitous. He's a dozy lump and he did forget to pick up the phone, and I did take it home because I thought it would be easier to return it to him myself rather than have to get back into the school to retrieve it. And then his mother's shop was closed and I did find out his address and I was going to drop it in some time, but then there were too many other things to think about and I forgot about it. Until I realised that it could be useful.'

'To frame him for the murder?' Rula Bartosz asked.

'To create a diversion. I didn't think he could actually be accused of the murder on that basis – and he wasn't, was he?'

'You didn't think about the anxiety it would cause his mother – and him?'

She gave a little sigh of exasperation. 'He's a useless lump of a boy. He's got no future anyway. I couldn't worry about him.'

'And Rebecca Clarke? What about her future?'

'I had to fight for my family. I couldn't think about her.'

Scott had interviewed a number of killers in the course of his career, but he thought he had never before felt such a reluctance to hear a story told. He glanced at Rula Bartosz and saw her brace her shoulders and sit up straighter, as if she was confronting an attack. He braced his own shoulders.

'Tell us,' he said.

Lucy Murano started speaking as though she was drawing up her words from a place deep and dark inside her. 'Ordering the phone cover was a mistake,' she said. 'It was my only mistake. Otherwise, it was well planned and well executed. I had followed Phil a couple of times on his early morning bike rides, and I'd seen him. The first time he just waved at the girl as though he happened to be riding past by a lucky chance. The second time he waylaid her – slewed his bike to a halt in front of her and started to talk to her, and I could see that she was uncomfortable. There was a moment

194

when he put a hand on her arm and I thought, *It won't be long before she makes a complaint. She'll tell her parents and we'll be finished.* I knew it had to be done there, by the river bank in the early morning, and I knew I was strong enough for it – all those karate classes weren't for nothing. And I had that phone, which gave me the perfect means to set up Josh Clements. But I had to have the phone cover because the body had to go into the river. I wanted to wash away any possible DNA. I was wearing protective clothing, of course. I was well covered from head to foot, I had gloves on, had a hat – and a mask. Isn't it odd that we can suddenly start going around wearing masks without advertising ourselves as criminals? I sent one phone message in advance and the other one the next day, then I followed Phil when he went out and I hid among the trees and watched them when they met. I could see him moving in on her. I wasn't a day too soon. She was on the verge of panicking, I thought – ready to rush home and spill to her parents. So as soon as Phil had gone, I made my move. I had found a piece of old electric flex in the shed along with all the other rubbish, and that did fine. A quick lasso with the flex – I'm taller than her, which helps – and I had her down. And I just kept twisting until she stopped twitching. And then the tricky bit was getting her phone out of her pocket, putting the cover on it and putting it back. There was always a danger that someone would come along, but I had a story prepared about having just found her lying there and trying to find out who she was et cetera. And then I rolled her into the river. It was really very easy. I'd removed the flex from her neck – I'm not sure why – and it was lying on the path, so I picked it up. There wasn't a plan actually to throw it into their recycling bin, but I realised as I was going back that I still had it in my hand, and I was near their house, so I dropped it in the bin. And that was that. Light the blue touch paper, retire and see what happened.'

195

'And you had no regrets?' Rula Bartosz asked.

'No.'

'When did your husband realise what you'd done?' Scott asked.

'I don't know. We never discussed it.'

Scott stood up. He wanted to be out of there. 'DC Bartosz, will you make the arrest?' he asked.

As Rula Bartosz put handcuffs on her and started reciting her rights, Lucy Murano said, 'It was a mistake to make a break for it, to try to leave the country. I wouldn't have done if it hadn't been for that journalist woman.'

Scott looked at her in surprise. 'Journalist woman?' he said.

'Said she was from the *Guardian*. Wanted to do an article on the impact of Rebecca's death on the people around her. She'd spotted Phil in the video about Rebecca that the family put out, and she wanted to interview him about how he was coping. And I knew he would give himself away. You saw how he was on that video – it was a pathetic performance.'

Scott frowned. 'Did this journalist give a name?' he asked.

'Yes. I'd never heard of her – we don't read the *Guardian*. Virginia something.'

'Gray?' Scott asked.

'Yes. Virginia Gray.'

'Of course,' he said.

Chapter Twenty-Eight

THE NEW NORMAL

5ᵗʰ June

It just didn't feel like home. Nonna and Nonno had been waved off on their plane back to Italy; the extra bed in Freda's room had been dismantled and stashed away; all her stuff, which Mum had put away in a box, had been brought out and distributed about her room where it belonged, and her favourite duvet cover was back on her bed. It should have felt as though everything was back to normal. She had played with Nico and let him try out his new conjuring set on her; she had reconnected with Ariel, their stolid cat, who seemed not to have been unduly bothered by her absence; and she had met up with friends for a walk, but all that did was bring back the lakeside walks and the crazy singing and the chats in the square, where there always seemed to be so much to say. Grace and Ruby texted her all the time, and sent her jokey little video clips, and that, strangely, felt like home. Now Eve, as she had promised, had sent her photos of the town square alight with candles for the D-Day celebrations. They had had celebrations here in their street as well – they had all stood on their doorsteps and sung that really bad song, but what was going on up in Carnmere just felt more real somehow. How could something that was happening hundreds of miles away feel more real than what was happening on your own doorstep? Eve had sent the pictures so that she could finish her art project. She had done her sketches of the town square through from March to May but she really wanted to finish up with the D-Day party and Eve had suggested that she could do it from photos. She wasn't sure if she could actually, but she would give it a go.

When she got out her other sketches to have a look at them, it occurred to her that maybe the reason that world seemed more real was that there was something sort of forbidden about it. Mum didn't actually want to hear about what she'd done while she'd been away. She didn't ask any questions and when Freda started talking, she often changed the subject. Ben said that Mum felt bad because she felt that Freda had been driven away because there wasn't room for her in the house, but Freda didn't think that was it. Mum didn't like to think that she had had a better time up in Carnmere with Granny than she would have done at home. Mum wanted to believe that home was always the best place, and that she, Freda, felt that too. Mum wanted her to say how glad she was to be home and how much she had missed it, but somehow Freda couldn't quite say it. Of course she loved them all and she had missed them, but the newness of everything up there had been exciting and, well, there had been an adventure. She couldn't talk to Mum about that – about calling the police, about actually rescuing someone from being attacked by her violent husband. Mum absolutely didn't want to know.

She had tried to tell Lily and Mia, her school friends, about the rescue drama but she'd had an uncomfortable feeling that they didn't actually believe her. They didn't say so but she felt sure that they thought she was making it up – or at least bigging it up. In a way, she couldn't blame them – it did sound super dramatic. But it had been. The truth was that dramatic things happened around Granny, and Freda didn't mind that. As far as she was concerned that was cool.

She sighed as she looked at her sketches. Were they any good? Had she really caught the atmosphere of the place? Now these pictures had become her memories and she couldn't say how true they were. Her history project had been a success, though. As she had hoped, sending it in early had meant that she got it back early, and Mrs Yardley had been really nice about it. She had called it *a proper piece of historical research*, and she had finished by saying that Freda had a career ahead of her either as a historian or in joining CID! When she had told Mum that, though, she'd said, 'Oh, for God's sake, not that nonsense,' and stuck her head into the pantry, pretending to look for something she didn't actually need.

It was quite weird, and talking of weird, something odd had happened to Granny. There was a lot of talk around at the moment about mental health, and the bad effects the lockdown had had on people, and Freda was quite worried. She had had a crazy email from Granny where she had talked about the woman who had been arrested for the murder of Rebecca Clarke. Freda knew all about her being arrested, of course, because there was a huge fuss about it on the news – especially because the murderer had turned out to be a woman, which was what nobody expected, but Granny rambled on about how she had been responsible for catching her, she had been the link, she had *gone undercover and smoked out the killer*, and although it *could never be revealed*, she was the person who was responsible for the arrest. It sounded completely nutty. How could Granny possibly have been an undercover agent when she was shut up in Carnmere with Eve and Colin? Freda was really afraid that she had gone delusional. Could it be that the lockdown had taxed her ageing brain beyond its limits? It was possible that her grandmother had gone round the bend.

Chapter Twenty-Nine

PERSONAL PROTECTION

20ᵗʰ July

I am no longer in thrall. My task is completed. The blanket is finished. I am released. Perhaps more pertinently, Eve is released from shielding, so there is no excuse any longer for my staying. Colin, I think, has been itching for me to leave ever since Freda went home. He has been increasingly taciturn and ungracious about the food we have cooked for him, and has spent more and more time in his study, to the clinking soundtrack of bottle and glass. I am quite pleased with the blanket. It doesn't bear close inspection – some of the early squares are not actually quite square as I seemed inexplicably to acquire extra stitches in the course of knitting them – but the overall effect is cheerful and warm, and that, I have to remind myself, is the point – it is not supposed to be an opportunity for showing off.

Do I want to go home? Yes, in some ways. I long for some solitude for a start – weeks of proximity to other people's feelings take their toll. So why am I reluctant? My own diagnosis is that the solitude offers time to brood and I don't want that because I don't want to think about the Muranos. It was all very well – the puzzle and the pursuit – and of course, the woman had to be stopped and punished, but I can't envisage a future in which those children will be all right. I suppose Philip Murano will take them away, and if he can't get another teaching job, he could probably get something in the PR line, but he's a weak man and he'll be carrying a load of guilt and I can't see how he's going to put the world back together again for two traumatised teenagers. I want to be so busy that I can't think about it, but I don't think that's going to happen.

We celebrated Eve's release from incarceration, she and I, by taking a walk into the town square and sitting outside in the sun, drinking coffee. It is amazing what an intense pleasure such a simple act can be – like breathing after you have been holding your breath. Eve was slightly wobbly, though, and she has been quiet and preoccupied ever since. I think she may be a bit afraid of a return to semi-normal life. She says she is worried about Elise. Things have not worked out well there; she is still in a women's refuge and her husband is in occupation of the house. This can't be right and yet it is what the law allows. It seems the police are not going to prosecute, even though Freda and I have offered ourselves as witnesses. They've got the hospital report on her injuries too. What more, exactly, is needed?

Yesterday I persuaded Eve to open up her studio by the lakeside. The tourists are beginning to drift back and she has still got a couple of months to sell some of the things she has been making while we have been immured, so we piled ceramics, cushions and sketches into their car and drove round to the far side of the lake. We parked illicitly in the car park for the Carnmere Manor Hotel, which dominates that area of the lakeside and offers the only parking, and then carried our boxes along the path to the studio, and I felt an extraordinary rush of emotions that I wasn't prepared for, preoccupied as I was with the practical business in hand. The previous summer, when Freda and I had stayed at the hotel, came back to me in all its horrors and knocked the breath out of me so that I had to put down my burdens and bend over until I could breathe again. A post-traumatic trigger, I suppose. This stretch of lake will forever be the place where I rush up and down in a state of sick panic because Freda is lost and there is no one to blame but me.

The studio, which is really just a wooden hut, smelt of warmed wood and dust and was quite intact – no one had tried to break into it. I cleared away the things that had been left out on display while Eve started to lay out the new stock. I carried the old stock into the workroom at the back, and as I was making space for it, I noticed that there was a bed in there alongside the kiln and the potter's wheel and all the other paraphernalia of Eve's craft.

I put my head through the doorway and asked, 'You don't ever actually sleep here, do you, Eve?'

She didn't look up from what she was doing and answered with her back to me. 'Occasionally,' she said, 'if I'm working late.'

'Working into the night?'

'Why not? Sometimes it's easier than going home.'

'Do you feel safe?'

She laughed, and then she did turn round. 'Oh, I feel quite safe here,' she said.

Her tone was odd and I didn't know quite what to say, so I ducked back into the workroom and did some more tidying up. When I came out again, she had finished laying out her wares and was eyeing them critically.

'I think they look lovely,' I said.

'Oh, that's all right then. As long as we think everything's lovely then it is, isn't it? Shall we have a cup of tea? I've brought a thermos.'

We sat at the little table outside to drink our tea, and neither of us seemed to have anything to say. Eve looked into her cup as though she could read the tea leaves and I sat looking out over the lake, and a thought came to me so powerfully that I couldn't suppress it, so that it came out in an awkward blurt.

'Are you afraid of Colin?' I said.

'The boys will be coming over from Ireland next week,' she said, and it didn't seem to be an answer to my question until she added, 'so that will be fine.'

She wasn't looking at me, still intent on her tea, and it felt too intrusive to look at her, so I kept my eyes on the lake.

'Why don't you want to be alone with Colin?' I asked.

'Well, I've been married to him for more than forty years, haven't I?'

She still wasn't looking at me, I could tell, and if I had turned to look at her, she wouldn't have met my eye.

'You're afraid of him, aren't you? That's what you and Elise have in common. Is that what made the bond between you?'

When she said nothing, I did turn to look at her, and she ducked her head to drink her tea although I was pretty sure that her cup was empty. Then it was her turn to look out over the lake.

'It's just a recent thing,' she said eventually, 'and it doesn't happen often. It started last year, with all the trouble over Ruby Buxton. He started drinking, and when he's been drinking he's sometimes... not himself. But he's still there really, Gina, and he's my husband, and I can deal with it.'

'Eve, you can't. You can't stay with someone who's violent to you, you can't stay with a man you're afraid of, you can't fill your house with visitors forever. How can I leave you and go home tomorrow if you're just waiting for the next time he's *not himself?*'

'I can tell. I can see when things are building up, and that's when I sleep here – until the mood has passed. You don't need to worry about me, Gina. I can deal with it.'

'You don't have to deal with it. Come down to London and stay with me. What's to stop you?'

'He needs me.'

I wanted to roar with exasperation and tell her that's what every abusive man makes his victim believe but for once I chewed my tongue, and we were silent in the car on the way back. I went upstairs as soon as we got in, with the excuse of more packing to do.

Now, this morning, we have eaten a silent breakfast and Colin has bid me a cool goodbye before retreating to his study. Gary is going to drive me down to London, and as Eve and I stand in the hall, surrounded by my bags and belongings, I know that I can't leave her like this. I turn to her and wrap her in a hug.

'Promise me,' I say, 'promise me that if he hits you again, you'll come down to me. They say there'll be another lockdown in the autumn, you know. Come to me.'

'All right. Yes. I promise,' she says, smiling at me with tears bright in her eyes, 'But I tell you what – an even better idea. If I tell him that you'll be back for the next lockdown unless he behaves himself, I think that should do the trick, don't you?'

'The nuclear option?' I say.

And when Gary arrives at the door and finds us helpless with weepy laughter, I don't attempt to explain.

Chapter Thirty

ONE OTHER HOUSEHOLD

*July 20*th

He tried the front door handle just in case she had actually forgotten to lock it, and then, when it did not yield, he lifted the loose flagstone beside the doorway. It infuriated him that she kept the emergency key there, in defiance of all security advice, but she had got away with it this time, it seemed – the key was still there, and it would take a very considerate burglar to rob a premises and then replace the key where he found it. He opened the door and immediately found himself ankle deep in mail and free newspapers. He kicked them aside to make a route into the kitchen, where he unloaded his shopping bags into the fridge, then took the empty bags back to the hall and refilled them with paper. Going through into the sitting room, he was relieved to find no flowers shrivelled and decayed in their vases or rotten fruit liquefied in its bowl. The strongest smell, in fact, came from his bags of mail, and particularly from the old newspapers. He sat down on the sofa, emptied out the bags and divided the contents into three piles – newspapers, junk mail and anything that looked as though it might be a meaningful communication. This third pile he neatened up and left on the coffee table, then he pushed the junk mail, into one supermarket bag and the newspapers into the other and took them out to the kitchen, where he opened the French doors into the garden.

He had exchanged text messages with Gary and he knew they couldn't possibly be back before four thirty. Feeling that he had done enough by way of tidying and was already in danger of being accused of interference, he ran the cold water for a while and then made himself a cup of tea, throwing away the open box of tea bags that had lain for months beside the kettle and unwrapping the fresh box that he had brought with the other shopping. He went into the garden with his mug of tea (which bore the legend, *Grammar Grumble: less milk and fewer sugar lumps*) and sat down on the peeling bench, which she still hadn't got round to repainting. The garden was a jungle; three summer months without any attention had left it free to go its own way and the result was riotous. Still, he thought as he sipped his tea, it was green and the birds were singing, and who said nature was supposed to be tidy, anyway?

When he had finished his tea he took out his phone, checked his emails and sent a couple of replies. Then he checked his texts. Nothing more from Gary. Restless, he paced round the little garden, and looking at the roses, half-strangled by bolder plants, he thought about picking some for the house. A rummage in the kitchen drawers eventually produced a pair of scissors, and he went out to disentangle the flowers, admiring the deep, velvety blooms and cursing their punitive thorns. Finding what looked like an adequate vase in the sitting room, he filled it with water and made an attempt to arrange the roses. It occurred to him that, at the age of fifty, he had never before arranged a vase of flowers. He had bought flowers occasionally for women – for his mother, for his hostess when invited out to dinner. *Never for Gina,* he thought, because there was always a good chance that there would be something wrong with them – out of season, too pretentious, past their best – and she would be ready to say so. He put the vase in the middle of the kitchen table and was rather pleased with the effect.

Going back into the garden, he resumed his pacing until he became aware of voices inside the house. She was back, and she had obviously invited Gary to come in with her. He waited, and soon he heard her go into the sitting room and say, 'What the hell? Someone's been in here.' Then she came through into the kitchen and saw him standing outside.

'David! You haven't come with bad news, have you?'

'Why would I bring bad news?'

'The girls? One of the children?'

'I'm the welcoming committee,' he said. 'I thought you might have a few re-entry problems coming down to Earth.'

Behind her, Gary loomed slightly awkwardly. 'Afternoon, David,' he called.

'Hi, Gary. Good drive?'

'Fine.' He turned to Gina. 'I'll be off. I've left your bags in that little room over there.'

'Sure you don't want a cup of tea?' she asked.

'No, no. I'll get back on the road. Leave you two to… reconnect. Bye, David. Take care.'

And off he went, with Gina calling out thanks behind him.

She came through into the garden. 'Welcoming committee?' she asked.

'Would you like a cup of tea? Or would you rather move straight on to the white wine?'

'Is there food to go with the white wine?'

'Smoked salmon, deli salads, ciabatta.'

'Then I think I'll leave the wine for a bit and have a nice cup of tea.'

She stood just inside the French doors, watching him as he made the tea. He saw her notice the roses on the table. 'A nice touch,' she said.

As he handed her a mug, he said, 'Don't worry, I'm not

necessarily expecting to share the wine and food, if you've been looking forward to a night on your own after months of togetherness.'

'Well, let's start with the tea, shall we, and see how we get on?'

'There are doughnuts. Do you want one?'

'Certainly.'

When she had demolished the doughnut and licked her fingers, she started talking. She launched into an account of Eve's neighbour and her dramatic rescue by Freda and herself, followed by a diatribe about the lamentable record of prosecutions in domestic abuse cases and the failures of the criminal justice system in general, for which she had decided to hold him personally responsible. She ran out of outrage eventually and moved on to Lucy Murano, hungry for all the details of her arrest and confession.

'How did she expect to get away with decamping to Italy?' she asked. 'Was she planning to move on to somewhere with no extradition agreement? Those countries are all drowning in COVID, aren't they?'

'She said her old boss from her job in the City had fixed her up with a job in Rome, no questions asked. She seems to have thought that she could get lost in Rome. She's something of a fantasist, I think – I'm not sure the job really existed – but she did borrow some money from her ex-boss, and spent it on an impressive wardrobe, I think. The outfit she was wearing looked as though it belonged on a film set.'

'The ex-boss sounds remarkably helpful.'

'Reward for past favours, I think.'

'Really?'

'And for silence about them.'

When they moved on to the wine and smoked salmon, she grew quiet, retreating into herself. She had something to tell him about Eve and Colin, she said, but not now.

He said, 'I really was prepared to leave you alone with this. I did realise that you'd had months of more company than you're used to and you could be yearning for solitude.'

'Well, none of the people I've been living with have been sleeping with me,' she said. 'Not even the dog.'

'How reassuring,' he said.

Some time later, as they were drifting off to sleep, she said, 'David?'

'Mm?'

'You know they say there'll be another lockdown in the autumn?'

'Mm.'

'I was just wondering whether, if so, you would like to be in my bubble.'

He laughed. 'You sound like we did at school, when we used to ask *D'yer wanna be in my gang?*'

'With girls, it's *Do you want to be my best friend?*' she said.

'That's one we haven't tried as a term to describe our relationship. *Best friends*, what do you think of that?'

'No, for heaven's sake! It's what divorced couples say – and I never believe a word of it. They think being *besties* makes them morally superior. They can't admit to all the base emotions that divorce dredges up – resentment, contempt, vengefulness, rage – or just good, honest hate.'

'OK,' he said. 'So maybe *bubble mates* will be a thing. What do you think?'

'Over my dead body,' she said.